The Jerr

Hidden Treasures

(A Paranormal Snapshot)

By Sherry A. Burton

Dorry Press

Also by Sherry A. Burton

The Orphan Train Saga

Discovery (book one)
Shameless (book two)
Treachery (book three)
Guardian (book four)
Loyal (book five)
Patience (book six)
Endurance (book seven)

Orphan Train Extras

Ezra's Story

Jerry McNeal Series (Also in Audio)

Always Faithful (book one)
Ghostly Guidance (book two)
Rambling Spirit (book three)
Chosen Path (book four)
Port Hope (book five)
Cold Case (book six)
Wicked Winds (book seven)
Mystic Angel (book eight)
Uncanny Coincidence (book nine)
Chesapeake Chaos (book ten)
Village Shenanigans (book eleven)
Special Delivery (book twelve)
Spirit of Deadwood (a full-length Jerry McNeal novel, book thirteen)
Star Treatment (book fourteen)
Merry Me (book fifteen)
Hidden Treasures (book sixteen)

Clean and Cozy Jerry McNeal Series Collection

(Compilations of the standalone Jerry McNeal series)

The Jerry McNeal Clean and Cozy Edition Volume one (books 1-3)

The Jerry McNeal Clean and Cozy Edition Volume two (books 4-6)

The Jerry McNeal Clean and Cozy Edition Volume three (books 7-9)

The Jerry McNeal Clean and Cozy Edition Volume four (books 10-12)

The Jerry McNeal Clean and Cozy Edition Volume five (books 13-15)

***Romance Books** (*not clean* - sex and language)*

Tears of Betrayal

Love in the Bluegrass

Somewhere In My Dreams

The King of My Heart

***Romance Books** (clean)*

Seems Like Yesterday

"Whispers of the Past" (a short story)

Psychological Thrillers

Storm Series

Surviving the Storm (book one, contains sex, language, and violence)

Sinister Winds (book two, contains language and violence)

The Jerry McNeal Series
Hidden Treasures

By Sherry A. Burton

By Sherry A. Burton
Published by Dorry Press
Edited and Formatted by BZHercules.com
Cover by Laura J. Prevost
@laurajprevostphotography
Proofread by Latisha Rich

For more information on the author and her works, and to sign up for the newsletter, please see www.SherryABurton.com

A special thanks to

I will forever be grateful to my mom, who insisted the dog stay in the series.

To my hubby, thanks for helping me stay in the writing chair.

To my editor, Beth, for allowing me to keep my voice.

To Laura, for EVERYTHING you do to keep me current in both my covers and graphics.

To my beta readers for giving the books an early read.

To my proofreader, Latisha Rich, for the extra set of eyes.

To my fans, for the continued support.

Lastly, to my "writing voices," thank you for all the incredible ideas!

Chapter One

O H N O

Four seemingly innocuous letters, but when put together, they could wreak havoc on one's day, week, month or—as Jerry would soon find out—life.

"Oh no!" April uttered once more as she handed him her cell phone.

The hairs on the back of Jerry's neck stood on end as he read the text from their contractor. > *Ran into trouble at the building site. Authorities contacted. All work stopped indefinitely.*

April pulled the phone back and looked at the screen. "We're not getting our house." The disappointment in her voice was palpable. Understandable as, freshly engaged, they'd lain in bed the evening before talking about the house and how excited they both were to be starting the next journey together.

"Don't go getting ahead of yourself," Jerry said, knowing the words were of little comfort.

"It says 'indefinitely.' What do you think it means?" April's voice was barely audible.

"It means the man's a coward who'd rather deliver bad news via text instead of making a call." Jerry struggled to keep his anger from showing as he reached for his own cell, intending to call the man on it. Before he could make the call, April's cell rang.

"It's Carrie," she said, swiping to answer. "Hello? Are you crying? Hang on, let me put you on speaker so Jerry can hear. Okay, now tell us what's going on."

"It's Houdini…I'm sorry," Carrie sobbed.

Jerry's anger dissipated as he watched the color drain from April's face. He took the phone from her trembling hand. "Carrie, this is Jerry. Calm down and tell us what's wrong with Houdini."

"Nothing. The dog is fine. It's just that I let him out before the builders arrived, and you know how much he likes to sniff the fresh dirt. Only today, he started digging. I didn't think there'd be a problem because they'd planned on starting to dig the basement today. I was within a few feet of him, and when I saw the trucks coming, I took hold of the leash to take him inside, but he didn't want to come. As the men arrived, he moved into a protective stance, growling at them as they got out of their truck."

April's eyes grew wide.

"Tell me he didn't bite anyone," Jerry said, praying it was true.

"No, he was just keeping them away from the bones," Carrie told them.

"His bones?" Jerry wrinkled his brow. "I've never known Houdini to guard his food."

"Not those kinds of bones, Jerry. It was a body! Or at least it used to be. All that is left is skeletal remains." Carrie sobbed. "We've lived here for years. How could we not know there was a body buried here? What if they think we killed someone?"

"That's just silly," April said, coming to her friend's defense. "They won't think that, will they, Jerry?" April looked at him, unblinking, as if expecting him to agree with her.

While Jerry's gut told him it was going to be okay, he wasn't about to weigh in on the situation until he had all the information. "Dan's text said he called the police. What did they say?"

"I don't know," Carrie sniffed. "They haven't gotten here yet."

"So, you haven't talked to anyone?" Jerry asked.

"Just Dan before I brought Houdini inside."

"Okay, good. Listen, my gut tells me it's okay, but maybe you should both stay inside and try not to talk to anyone until we get home."

"When will that be?"

"We're getting ready to leave Frankenmuth, so we're about an hour and a half out."

"What if the police want to talk to me?"

"Go to our house," April said and looked at him to confirm.

"That's fine. It's not like it's a fresh body. Take Houdini with you, and if anyone asks, you're taking him home."

"I need to calm down first. If I'm crying, they'll think I'm guilty." Carrie sniffed.

"Don't overthink it. They'll probably expect you to be crying. After all, they just found a dead body on your property," Jerry told her.

"Technically, it's on April's property," Carrie reminded him. "But that's neither here nor there; I'm the one who sold it to her, so they'll blame me."

"If anyone wants to talk to you, tell them the property belongs to April and let them know you expect us back shortly," Jerry replied. "Now, get going before the sheriff arrives."

"Way to throw me under the bus," April said the minute Carrie ended the call.

"No one is throwing anyone under the bus," Jerry told her. "You and I have nothing to worry about, as the property hasn't been in your name long enough for a body to decompose into clean bones."

"Then why tell Carrie to say anything at all?"

"To calm her down. The poor woman is so

rattled, she's liable to confess to murder without even realizing it."

"You don't think…?"

"No," Jerry said truthfully. "But I'd feel better if we can get going. If you could check on Max and try to hurry her up. I'm going to call Fred."

"Fred? That means you think this is serious."

"Not in the way you're thinking. But I guarantee Fred will know about this before we get home. To be honest, with Dan calling the police, I'm surprised we haven't already gotten a call," Jerry said, speaking to the fact that Fred Jefferies kept tabs on everyone who worked for him and often knew things before being told. As if on cue, Jerry's phone lit up, announcing Fred's call.

April pointed to Max's room and then left him to his call.

Jerry smiled and swiped to answer. "You're losing your touch."

"How's that?" Fred asked.

"You normally know what's going on in my life before I do," Jerry replied.

"Oh, I've known for a few moments now. I've just been waiting for you to do the right thing and fill me in."

Jerry doubted the validity of this statement. "Meaning you had someone running checks on unsolved missing persons in the area."

"How is it you didn't know there was a body

buried on the property? Isn't that precisely what I pay you to do?" Fred asked.

Jerry laughed.

"What's so funny?"

"I'm a psychic, not a bloodhound."

"You can't go anywhere without encountering a spirit. Why didn't you or Max know about this guy?"

"Probably because the spirit moved on."

"What about Gunter? Why didn't he find the body?"

"I imagine he wasn't looking for it."

"Let that dog know that, from here on out, he's to clue you in on any bodies in the vicinity that are not properly buried."

Jerry looked over at Gunter, who lay on the bed sleeping with his head on the pillow and his legs awkwardly lifted in the air. "I'll let him know."

"I hear it was the pup who found the body. Why him and not the father?"

"Houdini is a digger."

"So, you're saying he may have found it by mistake?"

Jerry didn't like speculating when it came to Houdini. "I wasn't there, so I don't know what prompted Houdini to dig."

"I do," Max said, coming into the room carrying her backpack.

Jerry considered muting the phone to hear her out, then decided to turn it on speaker when April bobbed her head. "Max thinks she can shed some light on this. Go ahead, Max," he said, waving the girl closer.

"Mr. Sinclair said if Houdini does good, we can cross-train him. I've been watching videos about cadaver dogs, and since I didn't have a body to hide, I've been using bones. I've buried them in the backyard so Houdini can find them." Max smiled a sheepish grin. "I've hidden some in the field near the school. He's gotten really good at finding them. Maybe he thought I'd hidden some at Carrie's house."

Fred's voice floated through the phone. "These bones you hid still had the meat on them?"

"Some of them. I boiled some clean to make sure he wasn't just smelling the blood. Plus, I started putting them in plastic to see if he could still find them. He did." She beamed.

Jerry had to admit to admiring Max's dedication to the dog's training. "Good job, Max."

"Sounds like Houdini has some bloodhound in him," Fred agreed.

Gunter took offense to Fred questioning the pup's lineage and emitted a grumbling growl.

"You keep me apprised of anything new, and I'll do the same," Jerry told him.

The screen blinked to show Fred had ended the call.

"At least with Fred on the case, we should be

able to get back to building the house soon," April said when Jerry pocketed his phone.

Don't say it. "Doubtful." *Way to go, McNeal. That should make for an interesting drive home.* Jerry hoisted his backpack over his shoulder and looped April's small bag over one of her suitcases while she took hold of the other. "Got everything?"

"Yes," both Max and April said at once.

"Good, let's hit the road."

***

Acting as if it were perfectly normal, Max opened the back door of the Durango and sang a greeting to Bunny, Elke, and Lina, who were all sitting in the third-row seat of the SUV.

Jerry loved that Max was so comfortable with her gift, acting as if seeing and speaking with spirits was perfectly natural. It helped that April believed in her special abilities.

He himself hadn't been as fortunate. While his grandmother encouraged his psychic growth, his parents didn't come around until a couple of years ago. As he watched Max climb into the backseat with Gunter, he wondered what his life would have been like if his parents had been more understanding of his uniqueness. *Don't go there, McNeal. You've already put all that to bed.*

He sighed and lowered the outside cargo porch attached to the trailer hitch. Setting the luggage on the grate, he went to work, strapping everything down.

"You sound flustered," April said, stepping up beside him. "You really are worried, aren't you?"

Jerry laughed to quell her unease. "I'm not overly worried. It's just when I put the back porch on the Durango, I thought we'd need it to bring home antiques, not hauling luggage so that the spirits we've collected along the way are comfortable riding in the backseat."

April eyed the luggage. "That's what I love about you."

"What?"

"We both know putting the luggage on the back porch isn't necessary, but since you know the spirits are here, you're trying to make them more comfortable."

Jerry shrugged. "If they're going to hang around, it's the least I can do."

April glanced inside the Durango. "How many are we up to now?"

Jerry followed her gaze and saw his grandmother's spirit had now joined Max and Gunter in the middle seat. "So far, there are only two more than we arrived with."

April raised an eyebrow. "So far?"

"Some people collect tangible things like clocks, figurines, and shot glasses, while you and I seem to keep adding to our spirit collection."

April laughed. "If we keep this up, we're going

to have to trade the Durango in on a tour bus."

Jerry frowned at the thought. "I rather like my Durango. What's so funny?" he asked when April giggled once more.

"I was just thinking of our tagline."

"Tagline?"

"*We go where the spirits take us.* Or we could get a panel van with *Let the spirit move you.* It will be great for surveillance, as people will think it's a moving van."

"Bad idea," Jerry said, opening her door for her.

April climbed in and fastened her seatbelt. "How come?"

"Because people are inherently nosy. If they think any of their neighbors are coming or going, they're going to want to check it out so they can be the first to tell everyone about the new arrivals."

Jerry closed the door, walked around the Durango, and climbed into the driver's seat. He continued the conversation as he drove. "Your heart is in the right place, but we have to know when to draw the line. Moving luggage is one thing. Changing vehicles to accommodate spirits would be like hanging out a welcome sign."

"You like helping them. I mean, it is literally your job. Would it really be that bad if word got out?"

Jerry recalled how many times in recent months the spirits had not only known how to find him but had also asked for him by name. Bunny was one of those spirits who'd found him, and yet he still had no idea what she wanted from him. "To be honest, there seems to have been a shift."

"Meaning?"

"I think word is already out." He wasn't saying it to scare her, but more to take her mind off of what was happening in Port Hope. "Tisdale found me, as did Bunny."

"Don't forget Lina and Elke," April said.

Jerry shook his head. "No, it was Bunny who told them."

"Who told two spirits, who told two spirits."

"That's about the way of it," Jerry agreed.

"For that many spirits in here, it seems pretty peaceful. Unless they're doing something you haven't told me about."

Jerry stopped for a red light. Glancing in the rearview mirror, he saw Granny holding up an aged bridal magazine as Bunny leaned over the seat. The pink-haired woman's eyes twinkled as she bobbed her head and commented on something on the page. He looked over at April. "I hate to break it to you, but I believe Granny and Bunny are planning our wedding."

"I'm sure they'll do a fabulous job of it."

Jerry glanced in the mirror once more, taking in Bunny's brilliant pink hair, Granny's floral house dress, and the yellowed bridal magazine. He focused on the road and addressed April. "I think you're going to want to take the lead on this one."

"You don't agree?"

"The bridal magazine is as old as they are. So, unless you want to look like a parrot in your wedding photos, I vote no."

Chapter Two

Unlike the trip over to Frankenmuth where April chatted happily, the drive east was filled with silence. From the front seat anyway, as the backseat held the excitement of Granny and Bunny eagerly making plans. Sisters Elke and Lina sat stoically watching Max, who wore her headphones and looked to be working on one of her drawings. That the sisters hadn't spoken let Jerry know the spirits were content. He only hoped April would be able to find a relative who would agree to take the heirloom before anything happened to disturb the status quo.

As they passed Walmart heading into Sandusky, Jerry pressed the brake to keep from plowing into the side of a minivan that pulled out in front of them. Though the driver continued at a snail's pace, April made no mention of it. Jerry looked over at his new fiancée. "You're awfully quiet over there."

"What? Oh, sorry, I was just thinking."

"About how happy you are to be engaged to me?" Jerry asked.

April smiled. "Of course I'm happy."

"Are you sure about that? You don't sound happy."

"Of course I'm happy. It's just been a lot to take in." April glanced in the back and lowered her voice. "First Randy, and now this. It's like the universe is trying to tell us something."

Jerry shook his head. "Don't let Randy take up space in your head. He's no longer a threat to either you or Max. Between breaking the restraining order, carrying a firearm, and at least two counts of attempted murder, he'll not be seeing the light of day anytime soon."

"Okay, what about the house? Dan's company is in demand. If he can't start on the house, he'll move to the next person on the list."

Hoping to avoid the traffic on the Lakeshore, Jerry turned at the light and traveled north on Elk Street. "Don't go getting ahead of yourself. We haven't even spoke to the man."

"There's no getting ahead of myself. Dan's text said 'indefinitely.' He's not going to sit idle when he has a whole string of people on the waiting list. Heck, he's probably already contacted the next person in line."

"If we can't build next to Carrie, we'll find another spot," Jerry said, hoping to calm her down.

"Yep, we'll just pick another spot at random and say, 'build here.' Oh look, there's a sign," she said, pointing to a real estate sign as they passed. "Maybe we should build in there."

Though he knew she was mocking him, building in Sandusky had its merits, as the town seemed to have good energy each time he'd been there. Since teaming up with Fred, he, as well as April and Max, had utilized the small airport north of town on more than one occasion. Not only could it accommodate a small Learjet, but word was the airport was in the process of expanding. Additionally, if April and Max had any issues while he was away, they would have not only access to local law enforcement but also the support of a small state police post located in the heart of town.

Jerry pulled into a driveway and headed back to the development April had just pointed out. Turning, he noted the wooded lots each looked to be at least a half-acre in size. Though the development was sprinkled with houses, there were plenty of undeveloped lots and enough trees to make each feel secluded. "Not bad," Jerry said, eyeing the properties separated by numbers nailed to trees.

April leaned forward in her seat, searching the landscape. "I thought you were worried about Houdini."

That she hadn't balked at the possibility was refreshing, as Jerry thought she'd veto the prospect outright since it wasn't close to Carrie. Jerry smiled. "Houdini is getting better with his training with each passing day."

"What about the neighbors?" April's voice was light as if pondering the possibility.

Jerry turned down an offshoot road. There was a sprawling brick ranch on the right that looked to sit on two acres of treed land, along with a two-story brick house at the end of the cul-de-sac. All the lots that lined the north side of the street were undeveloped and full of mature trees that reached high in the sky. Behind the tree-filled lots sat a vast field used for farming. Though there was no hint of the crop to come, the field looked to be freshly plowed. Jerry counted the parcels as he drove to the end of the street and wheeled the Durango around the circle. He stopped and rolled down the windows.

"Why are we stopped?" Max asked. "I thought we were in a hurry to get home."

Jerry pushed the button to kill the engine. "The bones are old. A few moments aren't going to make a difference."

"Jerry said if we can't build next to Carrie, we could maybe build here," April replied.

Jerry looked in the mirror to gauge Max's reaction. Though he was expecting an explosion of tears along with reasons why living here wasn't an option, Max merely stared out the window.

The undeveloped lots lined the entire north side of the street and around the corner that led out of the development. While he wasn't an expert, all told, it looked to be perhaps three or so acres. While smaller than their current five acres, the way the lots were laid out made the area appear larger. Jerry pointed out the lots to the north. "If we purchase them all, the neighbors will be a non-issue."

"What was that you said about not getting ahead of ourselves?" April said softly.

"I'm not trying to change your mind, and it isn't as if we need to decide at this moment. I just want you to know we have options. We could put the house in the center facing out, and no one would be able to see the backyard unless they were in the field." Jerry could almost picture the house they'd designed nestled into the woods. With its vaulted ceilings and wrap-around porch, it would be a hidden oasis nestled among the trees.

A tap on the window drew his attention. Bunny stood by the driver's side door. He rolled down the window.

She smiled. "I like it here. It's nice and quiet. I can sit in the rocking chair and watch the traffic."

Jerry took in the empty road. "There isn't any traffic."

"You're right. There's hardly any noise at all," April agreed.

He started to tell her he'd been speaking to Bunny when Lina appeared at Bunny's side.

"Yes, that would be just lovely. I vote we plant a small garden to the west."

Jerry opened his mouth to tell her that neither she nor her sister would be staying long enough to have a vote when Max handed her drawing pad over the seat. Jerry took the pad and marveled at what she'd drawn. "I know it shouldn't surprise me, but your gift is remarkable." He continued to study it with rapt fascination, knowing this was the reason Max hadn't balked at building here.

"What is it?" April asked.

Jerry turned the photo to show an amazingly close resemblance to the house they were planning to build. Instead of sitting on the property close to Carrie's house, Max's rendering showed the home nestled into these woods surrounded by large trees.

April's fingers traced the freshly drawn sketch. "Does this mean we aren't building beside Carrie?"

Not wishing to give her false hope, Jerry took hold of her hand and kissed the freshly placed engagement ring. "I'm pretty sure this is a preview of coming attractions…we could try to change it, if you want to look elsewhere." Even as he said the words, he knew the answer.

April left her hand in his as she turned and stared out the window once more. "No, I rather like it here. It's peaceful and speaks of new beginnings."

The words were no sooner out than several deer that had been camouflaged among the foliage until this instant stuck their heads up to see who'd disturbed their solitude.

April sighed. "We'll be taking away their home."

Jerry gave her hand a gentle squeeze before releasing it. He started the engine, and the small herd bounded off toward the back of the property, their white tails waving like flags as they continued across the open field.

Gunter whined an eager whine.

Jerry shifted into drive. "Let's see what's going on at the property and go from there. Just to be safe, take a photo of the sign on the way out. We'll call and set the wheels in motion, so we don't lose our spot with the construction company. And don't worry about the deer; if we build here, we'll leave as many trees as possible and plant more after the house is up."

***

Even with the detour, Jerry exceeded the posted speed limit and returned to Port Hope in under an hour and a half. In that time, April had called the realtor, surprising the man by telling him they wanted all the lots that lined the northeast corner of the development. After ending the call, Jerry laughed and told her that it was probably the easiest sale the man had ever made. He pulled up to the house, waiting as April gathered her purse. He looked in the mirror and saw Lina and Elke watching from the third row. Sighing, he placed the Durango in park.

"What are you doing?" April asked when he got out.

"Offloading some cargo."

"The bags can wait," she told him. "There's nothing in there I need right away."

Jerry lifted the back gate and pulled the frame containing Lina and Elke's fabric free. "That isn't the cargo I'm worried about," he said, handing her the frame.

Her brows knitted. "The sisters?"

Jerry nodded. "They've made it clear they go where it goes. I'd rather they stay here. I don't know what I'll be dealing with when I get there, and don't want to add to the confusion."

April looked at the Durango. "What about Bunny?"

"She and Granny disappeared as soon as I stopped. Something tells me they're already there."

"Okay. Come on, Max."

"I was thinking I'd take Max with me."

Max's eyes lit up. "Really?"

"Are you sure?" April asked. "What if the spirit of the bones shows up?"

Jerry leaned in for a kiss. "She's a forensic sketch artist. This is what Fred hired her to do."

"You want her to draw the bones?"

"With any luck, there'll be more to it than that. Don't worry, I promise to keep her safe."

"Maybe we should let Houdini go with her," April suggested.

"Not until he's officially on the job. Don't worry," he said once more. "Gunter's riding point on this one."

"Okay, you two go do your thing and this here mere mortal will go see how Carrie is holding up. I'm warning you in advance, there will probably be wine involved."

Jerry stepped around her, reached into the back and pulled out one of the bottles of wine they'd purchased in Frankenmuth. "This should hold you two until we get back."

"Only one bottle?" April's face was stoic.

Jerry lifted an eyebrow. "You're kidding, right?"

"Of course I'm kidding," April replied, "then again, more wine might help soften the blow about us not living right next door."

"We don't know that for sure," Jerry reminded her.

"Yes, we do," April said.

"Yes, we do," Jerry agreed.

***

April walked into the house as if being led to the gallows, knowing she was about to break her best friend's heart. Not only had the woman learned she had bodies buried on her land, but she was about to learn of their decision to move away. While a part of her wanted to wait until things settled down, Carrie was no fool, so it was best to rip off the Band-Aid and then drown their sorrows in wine.

Houdini greeted her with a frenzy of yips as soon as she opened the door. April stood behind the door frame to keep him from jumping on her before remembering to ask him to sit.

Houdini whined, then lowered to a sit, quivering as his tail drummed the floor.

"Hang on, Dude. Let me put these down before I break them. Being haunted is one thing. But the last thing we want to do is piss these two off." As the words spilled from her mouth, April wondered if the sisters had even followed her inside. She got her answer a second later when Houdini's eager whines turned into a menacing growl as he forgot his command and barked a deep, hackle-raised warning while stretching his nose toward the frame.

"It's okay, Dude. I know they're here."

"What's got him so riled?" Carrie asked, rounding the corner. That her friend was wearing her good apron told April everything she needed to know. It was Carrie who'd taught her the art of baking to keep her mind busy whenever she found herself stressed.

April smiled and sniffed the air. "Brownies or chocolate chip cookies?"

"Both," Carrie said, untying the apron. "It's a

good thing you're home. I was just getting ready to start in on blueberry muffins."

"How about we start in on cheese and wine instead?" April handed Carrie the wine and picked up the frame, which prompted a new round of hysteria from Houdini.

"I've never seen him act like that," Carrie mused. "Why doesn't he like the picture?"

"It isn't a picture," April said, turning it for Carrie to see.

"Oh, pretty. Is it a collage?"

"Of sorts," April agreed. "It's a sample quilt piece made from the dresses belonging to eight sisters."

Carrie peered closer and read the words within the frame. "*Love Overflows & Joy Never Ends In A Home That's Blessed With Family And Friends.*" She bobbed her head in approval, then frowned at the dog. "I like it. Why doesn't he?"

"Probably because the sisters are attached to it."

"Was that a statement or a fact?" Carrie asked, taking a step back.

"Both. Jerry left it here so the sisters wouldn't follow him to your house," April said. She walked into the dining room and removed a picture from the wall. Lifting the sister's frame, she placed it on the wall and adjusted it to level it. She looked about the room and spoke to the air. "I hope this will do. It's only temporary until we find its rightful owner."

Carrie stood just outside the dining room, arms crossed, rubbing her arm. “Do you think they heard you?”

“I’m sure they did. I think they are happy with the location for now, as their energy is better.”

“How can you tell?”

April nodded to Houdini. “He’s happy. It means he doesn’t feel a threat.”

“You mean they were threatening you before?”

“No. I don’t think so. I just think they were unsettled.”

“You’re pretty good at this.”

“I wish I was better. I really do want to help them,” April said sincerely.

“You could have fooled me.”

“It’s all smoke and mirrors,” April said. “I’m just repeating what Jerry told me. He went to check on things at the property. The suitcases are on the porch. Let me bring them in, then we’ll talk.”

Carrie followed her to the door and helped get the luggage inside. Once finished, they moved to the living room.

April sat on the couch. Houdini wasted no time jumping up next to her and all but climbing into her lap. April laughed as she sank her hands into the shepherd's fur.

“I dare say he missed you,” Carrie said.

“He misses Max, but I’ll do until she returns,” April corrected.

Carrie started to sit and stopped. "The ring! Oh, my goodness! In all the excitement, I forgot about you being engaged. Let me see it."

"It belonged to his grandmother," April said and held out her hand so her friend could see. "Isn't it beautiful?"

"Stunning! You must be on top of the world!"

"I am."

"Wait, you're engaged, and Randy's probably heading to prison for a very long time. Why don't you sound more excited? Is it the body? It is, isn't it? It's all my fault. I should never have allowed Houdini to dig."

Houdini looked up at the mention of his name.

"It's not your fault. They were going to start digging today. They would've found them anyway," April reminded her. She decided to press forward. "Either way, they've been found, and according to Max, we won't be able to build there. Don't be mad, but we ended up finding some property on the way home. Max showed us a sketch she'd been working on in the car and it was the same property. It's in Sandusky, so we won't be moving that far."

"Oh, thank goodness!" Carrie replied.

April couldn't believe her ears. Not only was her friend not upset, but she seemed practically giddy. "You didn't want us to build there?"

"It was okay when it was just you and Max. But then there was Jerry and the dogs."

"I thought you liked Jerry and the dogs."

"I do, but Mr. Land Baron is another story. I begged him to let me sell you five acres. He didn't want to sell his family land and only agreed because I begged and told him I didn't ever see you getting married and that you'd need someone to look after you."

"Why didn't you say anything before we had the land cleared?"

"It's your land," Carrie replied. "You bought it free and clear. It wasn't as if I could take it back."

"How about I sell it back to you?" April winked. "Though I might have to charge a bit more since I know how much you want it."

Houdini's head snapped up. Ears twitching, he scrambled from the couch, emitting a deep, throaty growl. The dog was practically quivering as he stared at April as if asking her permission.

"It seems he's not a fan of price gouging." Carrie laughed.

"No, it isn't that; something's wrong with Max." April hurried to undo the harness. Houdini wasted no time in backing out of it and disappearing.

Carrie drained the contents of her glass then reached for the wine bottle. She started to pour another glass then tilted the bottle instead.

Chapter Three

As soon as they started toward the property, Jerry felt the pull. He looked over at Max. "Do you feel it?"

Max bobbed her head. "I do."

Jerry smiled. "That's the pull."

"I've felt it before but didn't know what it was called," Max replied.

"I am not sure if that's the official title, but it's what I call it. Seltzer always referred to it as my Spidey senses."

"I wish we could still meet him."

"What do you mean 'still'? We're going to see him and June in two weeks."

"I thought we were going to have to cancel." Max shrugged. "On account of the bones and us moving and all."

"We're not moving until we have a place to move to. Besides, neither of those things should keep us from going. The only thing we need to worry about is getting Houdini certified so he can go with us. Your mom and I can help, but most of it will be on you since you'll be listed as his handler. It's a lifetime commitment, and you won't be able to stop the training even after he's certified."

"Maybe more," Max replied.

"More what?" Jerry asked.

"You said it's a lifetime commitment, but he's part ghost. That means he might be like Gunter and come back," Max reasoned.

Jerry glanced in the rearview mirror. Gunter smiled a K-9 grin, and Jerry realized that Houdini coming back was a real possibility. "You're right. Which is another reason to make sure he's fully trained in case something happens to him."

"You don't think anything is going to happen to him, do you?"

"No. Besides, you're closer to him than I am. If there were anything to worry about, you'd probably know it before me." It was mostly true, but there had been times when the person was too close to the situation to get a proper read. He thought of his friend Savannah and the time her wife was in danger. While he had picked up on the danger instantly, Savannah had been too close to the situation to notice. Still, he wasn't worried, as he didn't feel anything bad when thinking of Houdini. "Let's try something. Close your eyes and tell me what comes to mind."

"About Houdini?"

"About anything. Think of the pull you're feeling and tell me what you feel."

Max was quiet for a moment. "Sadness. I also see a turtle."

While he himself had picked up on a sadness along with a strong hostile, he'd not felt a turtle. "Keep going."

"Anger," Max said, confirming.

"Is the turtle mad?"

Max giggled. "No, it's the woman. No, he's a man. He just felt like a woman for a moment because of the long hair and makeup. I guess he's both sad and mad. His wife is only sad and wants everyone to go away."

"Where does the turtle fit in?"

"It's all around us."

Though he had asked in jest, Max's reply sent a tingle across the nape of his neck, which spread as they approached the turn to the property, and he saw vehicles lining the driveway. Jerry recognized a few as belonging to the construction crew; others remained a mystery. He bypassed the line and continued to the building site, which sat just to the west of the main house Carrie shared with her husband. Two police vehicles, a firetruck, and several others with official seals were parked in the drive and yard in front of Carrie's house. Seeing a few parked on Carrie's well-maintained yard angered him.

Max leaned forward and pointed toward the property. "That's Susie's car! I didn't know she was going to be here."

Gunter barked. Whining, he paced the backseat.

"Neither did I," Jerry said as he pulled up next to Susie Richardson's rental car and killed the engine. Susie was well-versed in dealing with the dead. Only as a mortician, her talents were normally reserved for the recently deceased. That Fred had sent her didn't come as a surprise. That neither Fred nor Susie had bothered to mention her coming left Jerry feeling a bit out of sorts.

He opened the door and slid out of the driver's seat.

Gunter jumped from the Durango, his nose sniffing the air.

"Are you coming?" Jerry asked when Max hesitated.

Max gave an apologetic shrug as she lifted the cover of her artist pad. "I need to…"

"No need to explain," Jerry said, cutting her off. "I get it. Everyone's gift works differently. Come find me when you're done."

Max blew out a relieved sigh as she picked up her pencil and lowered her head.

Jerry started to shut the door, then hesitated, thinking he should insist she walk with him, as something about Max staying in the truck bothered him. *Don't be ridiculous, McNeal; it's Port Hope. Besides, the place is crawling with cops.* He placed the keys in the driver's seat. "Do me a favor and lock the doors. The keys are in the seat. If you get too warm, start her up. Don't forget to lock it if you leave."

"Okay, Jerry," Max said without looking up.

As he started toward the building site where Susie stood talking to several men, Gunter moved to his side. Dan, the leader of the construction crew, saw him coming and hurried to greet him.

Gunter moved forward, placing himself between Jerry and the man.

Dan stopped abruptly, his forehead wrinkling as if pondering the reason he was unable to move forward.

"Any word?" Jerry asked, drawing his attention.

"I'm sorry, Mr. McNeal," Dan said. "I know you and April are eager to get this project underway, but my hands are tied until the scene is clear. Depending on how long it takes to resolve matters, I may have no other choice but to move to the next person on my list."

"How long?" Jerry asked.

Dan rocked back on his heels. "Like I said, my hands are tied until we get the green light to resume."

"I mean how long before you have to move to the next project?" Jerry clarified.

Gunter nosed the man's leg.

Dan moved to the side and brushed his pants. "I don't know. A couple of weeks."

"You're telling me you don't have a side project that can keep you busy for five weeks?"

Dan scratched his head. "We have a garage on the list. I might be able to move that up to keep the crew busy, but there's no way to guarantee this matter will be cleared up by then, and we'll have piddled around for nothing."

Jerry stood firm. "It won't be for nothing. You'll be given the green light to build."

"You can't be sure this land…"

"If not this land, then we'll move the building site. We have another parcel and need to bring in a crew to clear it before you start." Okay, so technically, they'd only spoken with the realtor on the way home and told him they wanted the land. But the man understood the rush and had promised if they signed the papers in the morning, they could close on the property within thirty days. He'd gone a step further by calling back and telling them with proof of funds and enough of a down payment, the current owner would agree to let them bring in a crew to clear the area for the house in advance of the closing.

"Where is the property?"

"Sandusky. It's forty-five minutes from here," Jerry said, hoping it wouldn't be an issue.

"That'll work." Dan smiled. "Don't look so perplexed. Most of my crew, me included, come from south of Yale. We'll all be happy to cut forty-five minutes off our drive. To be clear, you have six weeks to get the land cleared and ready to build on. After that, we'll move on to the next project."

"Understood," Jerry agreed.

"Good. Text me the address of the property, and I'll swing by and check it out on the way home and start filing the permits."

"Don't mind the signs. We haven't bothered to take them down yet."

Dan cocked an eyebrow. "Meaning you haven't actually purchased the property yet."

"Let's just say we made a gentleman's agreement."

"Six weeks, not a day more," Dan reminded him. "Providing we can get the permits in time."

"You just file the paperwork and worry about keeping your end of the bargain," Jerry replied. "The property will be ready even if I have to clear it myself."

Gunter tired of the man and sat scratching an imaginary itch.

Dan must have felt the energy shift as he took a step closer and lowered his voice. "If it were me, I'd forget about this place and focus on your other property."

"Oh?"

"See that redhead? She's DOD. Drove up in that 'Stang about ten minutes ago." Dan laughed. "Reminded me of something from a TV show. One moment, the guys were ogling her and the car, and the next, she was standing there barking orders."

"Where'd she come from?" Jerry asked, not letting on he knew Susie.

"That's the thing," Dan said. "She just showed up and started waving her badge, telling everyone to back away from the bones. She hasn't touched a thing. The way I hear it, no one knows who called her."

"You sure she's on the up and up?" Jerry asked, fanning the flame. "Anyone can purchase a badge on the Internet."

Dan's eyes grew wide. "Come to think of it, she did flash it pretty quick before returning it to her pocket."

Jerry chuckled. "I was just razzing you. I'm sure she's legit. Just to be sure, I'll go check her out," Jerry said.

Gunter stood and shook off the dirt, then sidled up to Jerry, staying by his side as they walked toward where Susie now stood talking to a Harbor Beach police officer. While Jerry had seen the man around, he'd never spoken to him. Aside from Carrie, no one in the town knew of Max and his position with the agency. He had hoped to keep it that way but knew that it was now unlikely. Avoiding eye contact with Susie, he addressed the officer. "Dan tells me there's a problem."

"You're McNeal?" the officer asked.

"I am."

The officer appraised him. "Your dog dug up a body, but something tells me you already know that."

"I'm aware my dog found some old bones," Jerry said, making the distinction.

"Yes, well, we don't know how old they are. We're hoping Ms. Richardson here can shed some light on that."

Jerry made a point of looking Susie up and down. "You're with forensics?" he asked, knowing she was not.

Susie extended her right hand as she flashed her badge with the other. "I'm with the Department of Defense."

"What does the DOD have to do with ancient bones?" Jerry asked.

A smile flitted over Susie's lips as she withdrew her hand. "Apparently, the call came over the wire. I was in the area, and my boss wanted me to come take a look."

Jerry glanced at the hole where Gunter stood, head lowered, sniffing the bones. "What have you found out?"

"Nothing."

"Ms. Richardson just got here," the officer told him. "She was just about to check them out to see if she could determine their age or origin."

Susie smiled at the officer. "Do you have a pair of gloves I could use?"

"Sure thing." The officer turned and hurried toward his cruiser.

Susie turned and walked to the hole. "I take it they don't know you're one of us."

"Nope. I was hoping to keep it that way." Jerry shrugged. "It's a small town. People talk."

"Why, Jerry McNeal, if I didn't know better, I'd think you are ashamed of your family."

Jerry raised a brow. "How many of your neighbors in Belfast know what you do?"

"All of them."

She was lying. He could feel it. "Liar."

"I'm not. You ask anyone who knows me what I do, and they'll tell you I'm a mortician." Susie smiled. "Some of the guys might use an adjective in front of that; then again, that just might be because I've threatened to cremate a couple that have gotten a little too fresh."

Jerry laughed. "I can see you saying that."

"Don't look now, but that cop seems overly interested in your ride," Susie said, nodding toward the Durango.

As the officer stooped and peered into the grill, Jerry pulled his phone from his pocket and sent Max a message telling her to keep the doors locked. "Maybe he's just a car buff and checking to see if she's got a Hemi," he said, pocketing his phone once more.

Susie laughed. "Or he can just look and see the vented hood, dual tailpipes and the word HEMI written on the side. My money says he just realized it's set up like a cop car, complete with lights and siren."

"That was my second guess." Jerry crouched over the hole and positioned himself where he could covertly watch the officer, who was now shielding his eyes, trying to look inside the Durango. The windows were deeply tinted, which meant the man's attempts would not be rewarded. Still, he was glad he'd told Max to keep the doors locked. The last thing he wanted was to have to explain the arsenal located inside. "What's your take on the bones?"

"They're clean, so they've been there for quite some time." Susie shrugged. "Honestly, I was biding my time waiting for you to get here. Listen, we both know Fred only rerouted me because I was in the area. He wanted you to have a backup in case this turns into something sinister. I was hoping you could give me a read on the situation."

"I haven't seen any spirits yet, but I can feel them watching."

Susie raised an eyebrow. "Them?"

"Definitely more than one body." Jerry motioned to where Gunter now stood, pawing the ground at a different location. "Can you see Gunter?"

Susie nodded.

"You'll find another body there."

The officer reached for the Durango's door handle. As he released it, he looked and saw Jerry watching. Losing interest in the SUV, he started in their direction in determined strides.

So much for staying under the radar. Jerry rose and took a step back when he neared.

As the officer handed Susie a pair of blue disposable gloves, his gaze trailed over Jerry.

Susie pulled on the gloves and squatted to inspect the bones.

"You a cop?" he asked Jerry.

And so it begins. "Nope."

"And yet you're driving an undercover police vehicle."

"I drive a government vehicle," Jerry corrected.

Susie looked up. "McNeal's with me."

The officer looked at both Jerry and Susie in turn. "She's your boss?"

"Technically, I'm her boss." Jerry flashed his badge, something he hated doing, as it always led to a new string of questions.

"Why all the cloak and dagger?"

Gunter moved in front of Jerry, watching the

officer.

Jerry shrugged. "I work for the DOD. Cloak and dagger is literally in the job description."

The officer held his ground. "What are you doing in Port Hope?"

"I live here. This is my property, remember."

"With a dead body. Is this an attempt at some kind of government coverup?" the officer asked.

"Bones," Jerry reminded him. "Buried long before we took possession of the property."

The officer focused his attention on Susie. "What's the story with the bones?"

Before Susie could answer, Gunter bared his fangs, emitting a deep growl. Now wearing his K-9 vest, the dog sprinted toward the Durango.

Jerry took off in a dead run even before Max's screams filled the air.

Chapter Four

Gunter pushed off with his back legs and disappeared into the side door of the Durango. The passenger door opened, and Max fell to the ground, spider-crawling backward for several seconds as her screams continued to fill the air. Not looking where she was going, she backed into Susie's car. The impact spurred her to her feet, and she took off in a blind run.

Jerry raced to catch up with her. Taking her by the shoulders, he spun her around, checking for signs of trauma. There was no blood or marks to show what had evoked such a panic.

"Max!"

Max's eyes were round, darting from side to side as she continued to scream.

"Max!" Jerry shook her, trying to break through her hysteria. "Come on, kiddo, calm down and tell me what's going on."

Susie stood just behind the girl, pistol in hand, surveying the surroundings for the threat. She looked at him for direction.

Jerry jerked his head toward the Durango. "Check the truck."

Susie nodded and headed for the SUV.

Max's screams turned into sobs as others gathered around.

"Jerry!" Susie yelled.

Jerry hesitated.

"MCNEAL!" Susie's voice was more insistent.

While still visibly upset, Max appeared somewhat calmer at the moment, so he waved the officer closer. "Don't let her out of your sight."

The cop bobbed his head.

Jerry hurried to where Susie stood, staring inside the passenger door at Houdini and Gunter. Both dogs were pressed between the two front seats, barking and snarling at something neither of them could see. Jerry's senses were pinging everywhere, but nothing told him what had everyone so upset.

Susie had her pistol trained on the SUV. "You want to open that back door, or should I?"

"Personally, I wish one of them could talk," he said with a nod to the dogs.

Susie laughed a nervous laugh. "Where's one of those spirits that hang around you when you need them?"

Jerry recalled what Granny had told him about asking for help. *Hello? I could use a little help with this one,* he said to himself.

Instantly, Clive Tisdale appeared at his side.

"Oh, now this could come in handy," Jerry said.

"What could?" Susie asked.

"I'll explain later. Clive, would you mind taking a peek inside there and see what's got those dogs so upset?"

"Don't need to go in; I already know," Clive told him.

"Do you mind sharing so I know too?"

"McNeal," Susie said, "please tell me you're actually talking to someone and haven't chosen this exact moment to have a nervous breakdown."

"I'm good. Clive's here."

"Clive?"

"Texas Ranger," Jerry said as Clive climbed inside.

"That's convenient. Tell me he has a gun."

Jerry recalled the Colt revolver in the spirit's hand. "He does, but I doubt it still works."

"Not for nothing," Susie said with a nod to the men who were inching their way closer, "but the locals are a curious bunch. We need to wrap this up before we get company."

"He's working on it," Jerry said, watching the spirit.

Clive exited the Durango and held up a white

cotton sack. "Caught the scoundrel."

"Scoundrel?" Jerry said, eyeing the bag.

"Snake. Pretty decent-sized one at that. Not one of yours. This one came from my side. It appears someone's trying to send you a message."

Jerry looked through the glass at Max. "I don't think I was the intended target."

"Target?" Susie repeated.

Jerry held up his finger to silence Susie and addressed Tisdale. "I appreciate the assist. Any chance you can find out who's responsible for this?"

"I'll look into it." Tisdale tipped his hat and disappeared, taking the snake with him.

Jerry lifted his arm, pretending to throw something, then opened the front door, petting Houdini to settle the dog. As he did, he saw the sketch Max had been working on. "Hey, Richardson."

"Yes?"

"Situation neutralized. And just so you know, your bones are Native American."

Susie stuffed the pistol in her waistband. "You sure?"

"I'm sure." Jerry showed her Max's drawing, which showed several Indians standing over the bones. He closed the cover on the sketchpad and placed it on the dash. Jerry clapped his left leg. "Houdini, heel." The dog jumped down, circled Jerry, and attached himself to Jerry's left side.

Gunter followed suit. As they cleared the front of the Durango, Houdini saw Max and started forward.

"Houdini, heel!" Jerry repeated. Houdini whined but stayed in place as Max ran to them. Jerry wrapped his right arm around her and pulled her close. She'd stopped crying but still breathed the occasional ragged sob. "Are you okay?"

"Is he gone?" Max's voice broke with the asking.

"The snake's gone," Jerry assured her.

"What about the Indian?"

"What Indian?" Jerry asked.

"What Indian?" Susie repeated.

"We'll discuss this later," Jerry replied. He felt Max's shoulders slump and instantly regretted they hadn't had more time to talk about it. Houdini growled as several men approached.

The officer looked them over. "She okay?"

Jerry decided to stick as close to the truth as possible. "Just scared. It appears we picked up a hitchhiker. A snake," he clarified when the officer looked toward the Durango.

"Where is he now?"

Jerry laughed. "Probably halfway to Canada as hard as I threw him."

"Just how does one get a snake in their vehicle anyway?" Dan asked, eyeing the Durango.

"We had the doors open earlier while loading it. Might have gotten in then. We were parked under a tree," Jerry added when the cop started to object.

The cop turned his attention to Max. "You sure it didn't bite you?"

"No, it just scared me," Max said, going along with the ruse.

"I have information about those bones," Susie said, pulling their attention away from Max. She started walking toward the dig sight, and the men followed.

Jerry waited until they were out of earshot before releasing Houdini's harness. The dog sidled up to Max, who stooped and buried her face in the dog's fur and sobbed once more.

"You want to talk about it?" Jerry asked when her sobs finally subsided.

"You don't believe me, so what's there to talk about?"

"Of course, I believe you," Jerry insisted.

"Then why didn't you tell them?"

"Max, not everyone is going to believe in what we do."

"But you have a badge, and you're the lead paranormal investigator."

Jerry picked his words carefully. "I am. And I could care less what anyone thinks about me, but I did that to protect you. We live in a small town, and people talk. Not everyone will believe us, even with the badge."

"I don't care what anyone thinks, and you shouldn't either. Maybe it's time for them to know.

You're here because you told people you had the gift. It's the reason Carrie told Mom to write to you. How do you know telling them won't help more people accept their gift?"

Jerry smiled. "You know, you're a pretty smart kid."

"I'm not a kid. I'm a forensic sketch artist for the Department of Defense, and those bones belong to the Native Americans."

"You're right," Jerry agreed.

"Are we going to tell the police officer?" Max's voice was hopeful.

"Susie is telling them about the bones," Jerry said. While he admired her determination, he wanted all the facts first. The man had obviously said or done something to frighten her. He was about to ask what it was when April's Durango sped down the driveway. Jerry looked at Houdini and sighed. He'd been so caught up in things, he hadn't stopped to realize Houdini hadn't come with them and that April must have released him when he alerted to Max being in danger.

April jumped out of the SUV and raced toward them the second it stopped moving. Carrie followed at a slower pace.

"She's okay," Jerry said as April gathered Max in her arms.

April pulled away, inspecting Max to be sure. "What happened?"

"We were just getting into that." Jerry looked at Carrie. "Do you mind if we use the house? It will be more private."

"Of course," Carrie replied, leading the way.

Jerry retrieved Max's sketchpad and followed them to the house. Once settled inside, Jerry told them about hearing Max scream and summoning Tisdale, who helped eradicate the snake.

"Are you sure it didn't bite her? It didn't, did it?" April asked, looking at Max.

"It didn't bite me," Max assured her.

"How did the snake get inside the Durango?"

"We were just getting to that when you showed up," Jerry said. "Max, please tell us what happened, starting with when I left you."

All eyes turned to Max, who sat with her arms crossed. Houdini sat on the floor, leaning against her legs while Gunter stood guard over both.

"It's okay," April said when Max exhaled a ragged breath. "You don't have to be scared anymore."

"I'm not scared. I'm mad," she said, looking directly at Jerry. "I figured everything out, and Susie will get all the credit."

Max's anger came as no surprise, as Jerry could feel it from across the room. "From the beginning," Jerry urged.

Max jutted her chin. "I could feel them all around me the moment we got here."

April shuddered. "You felt the snakes? You're saying there's more than one?"

"Let her finish," Jerry said, urging Max on.

"No, I didn't know about the snake. I felt the spirits. They were all around me, and they wanted me to draw them."

"How'd they know you could draw?" April looked at Jerry. "It's a serious question. If these spirits are going to prey on my daughter, I want to know how it works."

"I don't know how it works," Jerry told her. "The spirits just know who can help them."

"You were there. Why not you?" April pressed.

"Because they knew Jerry couldn't help them," Max said before he could reply. "They are Indians and knew Jerry couldn't understand them."

"And you can?!" April asked.

"No, that's why they got mad."

"Okay, so let me get this straight, we have an Indian buried on our property?" Carrie said.

"Indians," Max corrected. "More than one."

Jerry patted the air with his hands. "They are Native Americans. Please, everyone, let Max finish her story before anyone else comes asking more questions."

"I started drawing the one I saw, and then others appeared. At first, they were just in here," Max said, pointing to her head. "I could see them standing around the bones and knew they were sad the bones had been dug up. The bones were of a young boy, maybe around my age. But I knew there were more around him."

"A burial ground," April said softly. She looked at Jerry. "Sorry."

"I drew it like I saw it in my head and was getting ready to take it to Jerry when the chief appeared outside my window. He said something, and I told him I couldn't understand him. His eyes grew dark, and he said it again. I didn't know what he was saying, but I knew he was mad. I could feel it. He shook his hand at me and yelled it again, only this time, he was holding a snake." She lifted her hand to demonstrate. "I wanted to get out to go find Jerry. When I reached for the door, he threw the snake at me—right through the glass. I think I swung at it because it flew into the backseat. That's when Houdini showed up and scared the chief away. Gunter was there a moment later."

Jerry watched as Max absently caressed the dog. "Houdini got there first?"

Max nodded.

"Why not Gunter?" April asked. "He was already here."

Hearing his name, Gunter tilted his head.

Jerry smiled. "It's a positive sign. It shows how connected they are."

"You mean Houdini felt her?" April asked.

"Possibly," Jerry agreed. "That, or she mentally

called him. Either way, she was in trouble, and he responded."

"Good boy, Houdini," April said, looking at the dog.

Houdini's tail beat against the floor, but he stayed next to Max.

"So, now what?" Carrie asked. "No offense to the Native Americans, but I can't have angry spirits throwing snakes at people on my land."

"I'm pretty sure they think it's their land," Max replied.

"I think Max is right," Jerry agreed. "But we need to figure out how to talk to them so we can make peace."

April giggled, then covered her mouth. "Sorry, you know I always giggle when I'm nervous."

"It will be okay." Jerry said, pushing off the couch. "I'm going to check in with Susie and see where we are with the authorities."

Max stood, and Houdini jumped up, ready to follow. "Are you going to tell them about me?"

"Only as a last resort," Jerry said, repeating his earlier words.

"It's not fair," Max fumed.

"Neither is having a whole town turn on you because they think you're a nut job," Jerry said firmly.

"I told you, I don't care what people think," Max said, standing firm.

"Maybe not, but I still want to test the waters before launching the boat." Jerry took a breath.

Max turned away without commenting.

Jerry sighed and softened his tone. "I am not ashamed of what we do, and I get what you said about helping others. But I've been dealing with this a lot longer than you. When people find out what you can do, they expect things from you. When you can't give them what they want, and trust me, it will happen, they will turn on you."

Once again, Max failed to respond.

Jerry looked at April, who merely shrugged. He sought out Gunter, who sat looking at him as if to say, *You've promised to guide her. Figure it out.* Jerry started for the door and hesitated. "Aren't you coming, Max?"

Max's eyes grew wide. "You mean you want me to come?"

McNeal, for a smart man, you can be pretty dumb. Jerry smiled. "Of course I want you to come. I'm not trying to exclude you. I'm trying to protect you."

Max started to bring her sketchpad and stopped. "Should I bring this or leave it here?"

"Bring it. You might need it."

Max scooped it up and hurried to the door as if afraid he would change his mind. From the corner of his eye, he saw April lean across the chair and give Carrie a high-five.

Chapter Five

Susie stood next to her rental, talking on the phone. Everyone else had either left the property or was in the process of leaving.

A horn honked. Jerry turned to see Dan sitting in his pickup with the engine idling. The man lowered the window and waved them over.

Jerry sighed and headed to the truck.

"Are you okay?" Dan asked, directing the comment to Max.

Max gave Houdini the command to sit before answering. "Yes, sir."

"Good to hear." Dan craned his head out the window. "That's a good-looking dog you've got there. A brave one too. My dog probably would have tucked tail and run."

While Houdini exhibited his best behavior, the

same could not be said for Gunter, who took this moment to appear inside the cab of Dan's truck. Hovering over the man, he sniffed his ear.

It was obvious to both Jerry and Max that Dan could not see the ghostly K-9, and his only reaction was to bat at the intrusion as if he were waving off a pesky fly. "I need the address of the other property so I can check it out on the way home."

Jerry took out his phone, pulled up a photo of the sign, and showed it to the man.

Dan bobbed his head. "I know where that is. Which lot are you buying? Just need it for reference if you're sticking with the same design so I can make sure the house will fit."

Jerry smiled. "The house will fit. We're buying every available lot on the northeast corner."

"Alrighty then. Sounds like we're building you a house. The only question is where. Give me a text in the morning and let me know if we are moving forward on this place or the new property so I know whether to apply for the permits." Dan looked over his shoulder and swatted the air. "Blasted gnats."

Jerry smiled. "Leave your window down, and it will probably be gone before you hit the pavement."

"Unless I kill it before it leaves." Dan swatted the air as he started down the long driveway.

Gunter appeared in front of them. Houdini wiggled a greeting.

Jerry looked at Gunter, who smiled a K-9 smile.

"I hope you're proud of yourself."

"He looks proud to me," Max agreed.

"He looks like a pain in the…"

Susie approached before he completed his sentence. "Good news."

While good news would be welcomed, the creeping sensation on the back of Jerry's neck told him he was unlikely to get any. "I'm listening."

"There are no regulations on Native American bones."

Jerry frowned. "I'm not following you."

"If the bones would have belonged to anyone else, you would have to jump through a lot of hoops. Sadly, there are no regulations on Native American bones found in the United States, so the landowner is free to do what they want with them."

"You mean they can just throw them away?" Max's voice held a mixture of shock and intrigue.

"Technically, yes," Susie replied. "Although I think it would be better to relocate them."

Gunter growled a low growl. Houdini lifted his head, sniffed the air, and joined the warning.

Houdini strained to move forward as Max dug in her heels and held firm to the dog's leash. "He's here," she whispered.

Jerry had felt their presence even before the dogs alerted. "It's okay, Max. The dogs won't let anyone hurt you." While he wanted to add that he would protect her as well, he knew the dogs were better suited for the task.

Susie cleared her throat. "Okay, for those of us who seem destined only to see the occasional spirit and are otherwise limited to shadowy forms, would one of you please tell me what's going on?"

Max pointed to the spirits standing near the hole. "The chief is here, and he brought his friends."

Slowly, the picture Max had drawn came to life, right down to what the entities were wearing. "Max, show Susie the photo."

Max uncovered the illustration she'd drawn and showed it to Susie.

The woman's eyes grew wide. "Don't they look like an ominous bunch?"

"That's because they aren't happy," Max said.

While Jerry wanted to tell them it was probably just their way, the energy surrounding the spirits told him Max was right. The spirit Max referred to as the chief wore a buckskin outfit. His hair hung loose to his shoulders and was covered by an ornate headdress made up of feathers. Leather strips trailed both sides of his head and continued downward, woven with a mix of beads and brightly colored feathers. A large bear claw necklace circled his neck, while a thick bone pierced the underside of his nose. There were white and red stripes painted across each of the man's cheeks. His shirt was extremely detailed, with a wavy design painted on the shoulders, trailing along the arms. The design was carried along the outer seam of the pants. The two other men wore the same buckskin, only theirs was much less ornate. The bear claw necklaces had fewer claws, and neither man wore a headdress. What each did have was a fair-sized tomahawk that looked sharp enough to do some serious damage.

The women's hair was in braids, and they wore beautifully embroidered white leather dresses adorned with brightly colored beads. The boy, who looked to be around Max's age, wore a painted buckskin adorned with feathers that matched those sticking from his hair.

Susie moved closer to Jerry. "How many are there?"

"Six that I can see. Three men, two women, and a young boy, just like in Max's drawing, but I get the feeling there are more." He looked at Max for confirmation.

Max nodded. "I feel it too."

Both dogs barked a warning as one of the men broke from the group, made his way to where they stood, and said something in a tongue none of them understood. Jerry shook his head. "I can't understand you."

The man turned and spoke to the small group that had appeared with him.

The chief responded, and the brave took a step toward Max.

Both dogs moved in front of her, blocking the

spirits' way.

"I can see them!" Susie exclaimed. "All of them!"

"I'm not sure that's a good thing," Jerry replied.

"Oh?" Susie's voice was calmer now. "Why not?"

"It means their energy is palpable."

"What does that mean?" Max asked.

"It means they might do something to get our attention," Jerry replied.

Max gulped. "Like throwing snakes?"

Jerry nodded. "They've done it before."

"Come on, Jerry, you have to have something in that bag of tricks of yours," Susie whispered.

"I'm not a magician. Besides, something tells me they won't be impressed with parlor tricks."

"What about calling that ranger friend of yours?" Susie asked. "He helped before."

"Clive? Maybe? Yo, Clive, if you're not too busy, we could use a little help here," Jerry said, willing the man to show himself.

Tisdale appeared, took in the situation, pushed back his Stetson, and furrowed his brow. "What in the blue blazes have you gotten yourself into now?"

"It's a long story, and I'll be happy to fill you in when things settle down," Jerry replied. "For now, I was wondering if you could maybe translate for us?"

Tisdale laughed. "You're kidding, right?"

Jerry shrugged. "It was worth a shot."

"Shot? Now that I can do," Tisdale said, pulling out his pistol.

The brave's eyes narrowed. As he raised his hand, he pulled the tomahawk from his waist.

Gunter now wore his K-9 vest, his woofs filling the air. Houdini followed his ghostly father's lead, challenging the spirits and pulling Max forward in the process.

Jerry grabbed hold of Max's arm. "NO!" He raised his hands, patting the air in a feeble attempt to calm everyone. "We are NOT doing this."

Susie took hold of Houdini's leash to help restrain the dog.

As if things weren't chaotic enough, Bunny took that precise time to materialize. She took in the scene and clapped her hands. "Oh, goodie! I just loved playing Cowboys and Indians with my brothers when we were kids. Only we never had costumes like that," she said, eyeing the natives.

"This isn't a good time, Bunny," Jerry said, struggling to remain calm.

Bunny's hands flew to her chest as her eyes grew wide. "You mean this isn't a game?"

"No," Jerry said. As he spoke, he realized the brave had lowered his weapon and was staring at Bunny as if she had two heads. Jerry wasn't sure if it was the spirit's pink hair or if he thought she was touched. Either way, the unlikely spirit had succeeded in deescalating things.

"Perhaps I should go," Bunny said.

"No, your being here seems to have helped."

"Oh." Bunny giggled. "Then I'd better talk to them."

"You speak Indian?" Max's voice was full of awe.

"A little. At least, I think so." Bunny stepped forward and raised her right hand. "How."

*Of all the hare-brained…*Jerry reached for the woman's arm to pull her back. The gesture was for naught, as his hand passed right through her.

Tisdale took the initiative and pulled her back. "Woman, you're going to get them all killed. They don't need you making a fool of yourself. They need someone who can speak Chippewa."

Bunny smiled. "Chippewa? Why on earth didn't you say so?"

"You're telling me you speak Chippewa?" Tisdale said.

Bunny shook her head. "Oh, no, not me. But Elke can."

Jerry fought the urge to look for a hidden camera. "Elke?"

"I can what?" the spirit said, appearing beside him.

"Speak to them," Bunny said, pointing.

Elke turned. As she did, her skirt brushed against the ground, sending up a slight spray of dirt. She summoned Jerry to her side and then continued walking to the small group, speaking slowly as she neared.

While Jerry didn't understand what she was saying, it was obvious the natives did. The energy surrounding the dig site grew calm. Even the dogs' barks subsided, though they continued to emit low growls. The chief did the talking, motioning to the boy and then pointing to the ground. A moment later, he sent his hands wide before growing silent once more.

"This man's name is Noodin. He and his family came over the great water to Turtle Island. It's the name they use for this land. They liked it here and often made trades with the men who would venture here. Each new season, they made a trek back to their homeland to further trade for supplies. Their last journey home was plagued by a great storm. They'd barely made it to land when a bolt of lightning came from the sky and hit the tree the boy was leaning against. Instead of burying him near the great water, they brought him here for his mother to watch over him." A sadness touched Elke's eyes. "The mother had died while they were gone. The son had braved the storm to tell his father. The boy was buried next to her. It is the mother, Orenda's grave you have disturbed."

"It wasn't us," Jerry said. "It was the dog."

Elke took in the cleared land. "This is where you plan to build your home?"

"It was."

"You do not wish to build here anymore?"

Jerry shook his head. "Considering the circumstances, I think it would be best if we did not."

Elke turned, relaying Jerry's message to the chief.

Noodin growled his response and pointed to the exposed bones.

"Tell him we will cover his wife," Jerry said without waiting for Elke to translate.

Elke relayed the message.

The chief spoke, his words once again coming out in angry tones.

Elke turned, looking at Jerry as she spoke, only the words were for the chief, not him.

The chief studied Jerry for a full moment before speaking in softer tones.

Elke smiled at Jerry. "Noodin wanted to know how I could be sure you are a man of your word. I told him about my mother's quilt piece and how you gave up something you loved to help me return it to my family. I left off telling him that you haven't fulfilled that part yet. He agreed you are a man of your word and wants to show you where he and the rest of his family are buried."

Jerry glanced at the chief. Hoping he wouldn't have to travel far to find them, he nodded his head.

The chief disappeared and reappeared a short

distance away. Within a few seconds, others appeared in the clearing where the house was set to be built. Gunter sniffed the air but remained silent. From nearby, Houdini barked, then quieted when Max reprimanded him.

Jerry took in the sight, counting just over a dozen spirits standing in place, and realized how close they'd been to building their house on ancient burial grounds. "Tell them we will not further disturb them. Wait," he said before Elke could translate. "Ask him if they would mind if we planted trees at their graves."

"He said that would be most honorable since your people cut down the ones that were already there."

"My people?"

"The white men."

Jerry thought of his discussion with Max. "Ask him if his people prefer to be called Native Americans or Indians."

Elke raised an eyebrow. "Those are names given to them by the white men. They prefer to be called by their name or tribe."

"Chippewa?"

The chief appeared in front of him and smacked his fist to his chest. "Anishinabek."

The gesture caught Jerry by surprise. "You can understand me?"

Elke spoke for him. "No, he just understood the

word 'Chippewa' and wanted to clarify who they are."

"Anishinabek," Jerry repeated.

Noodin nodded, then disappeared. One by one, the others followed him into the unknown.

"That was so cool!" Max said, running toward him.

Jerry looked at Susie, who joined at a slower speed. "Did you see it all?"

"Nope. Not after their energy calmed. Max gave me a play-by-play, so that helped. Is Elke still here?"

"Yep," Jerry said, nodding to where the spirit stood.

"Can she hear me?"

"She can."

Susie turned to where Jerry had indicated. "How is it you knew their language?"

Elke moved forward.

"I can see her," Susie said, sucking in a breath.

"That's because she wants you to," Jerry told her.

"My father, along with others from our church, came here with hopes of civilizing the Indians. Most didn't want any part of it, as they had their own beliefs. There were a few who were fascinated enough to learn our language, so they hung around. One of them had a son, a young brave, who liked the color of my hair. He taught me many things." The color rose in her cheeks, and she promptly disappeared.

Susie cocked her head to the side. “Wait… spirits can blush?”

“She must have been embarrassed that the Indian taught her his language,” Max surmised.

“Yep, I’m sure that was it,” Jerry agreed. He smiled at Susie. “I guess you’re officially done here?”

She nodded. “I’m going to stop by the police station and file an official report declaring the bones to belong to Native Americans, and then the agency will follow up with any paperwork. If I hurry, I can still make my evening flight.”

“You sure you don’t want to stay a bit?” Jerry asked. “I’ll give you the three-minute tour of our city.”

“Nope. It’s too lively around here for my tastes.”

Jerry chuckled. “You just don’t want to be there when I officially tell April we aren’t going to build here.”

Susie waggled her eyebrows. “You got that right.”

“Mom already knows we’re not building here,” Max said.

“You already told her?” Jerry asked.

“No, it was Carrie. She told Mom they didn’t want us to build here now that you’re marrying my mom.”

Susie clamped a hand on Jerry’s shoulder. “Don’t take it so bad, McNeal; the husband is always the last to know what's going on."

"They're not married yet," Max told her.

"They're married enough." Susie smiled at Max. "Think you can find us a shovel?"

"Sure thing," Max said and took off with Houdini running at her side.

"Have you two set a date?"

"There's been so much going on, we've barely even talked about it." Jerry looked up and saw Granny standing beside his Durango, talking to Bunny and Tisdale. He sighed when she waved him over.

"Problem?" Susie asked.

"Granny's calling me over. Bunny and Tisdale are with her. They seem to be conspiring."

Susie laughed. "You know, you lead some life, McNeal."

"Yep," Jerry agreed. "I'm one lucky man."

Chapter Six

Tisdale and Bunny disappeared before Jerry reached the trio. Jerry didn't mind, as it would give him the opportunity to speak with his grandmother alone. "You're a little late to the party," he said, noting his grandmother's earlier absence.

"I was there."

This caught Jerry by surprise, as he hadn't felt her presence. "You were? How come I didn't know it?"

"Because I couldn't have helped you." She sighed. "That's what I've been trying to tell you. There is so much more to the gift than always relying on me to lead the way."

She hadn't seemed to mind helping him before. He wondered what had changed. As soon as the thought occurred to him, Gunter appeared at his side, leaving him to further wonder if that was the message his grandmother was trying to convey. "Gunter is fantastic. I cannot imagine my life without him, but I needed more help than he could provide today."

"Gunter is but a piece of the puzzle. Your own private alarm system, if you will. But each spirit you meet along the way becomes a part of your arsenal and will help when called upon."

"Each spirit?" Jerry repeated.

"That's right."

Jerry skimmed through the catalog in his mind and picked one at random. "You're saying Ashley Fabel is an asset?"

"No, but her brother is."

"Mario Fabel is a crime boss," Jerry reminded her.

"Remember the case you were working in Texas? Do you really think Mario Fabel just happened to reach out to you with the exact information you needed at the precise time you needed it?"

Jerry thought of the seemingly random conversation he'd had with the man. "It was interesting timing. He isn't a spirit, though."

"No, but Ashley is."

"You're telling me she sent him?"

Granny nodded. "Think of the people you meet along the way as building blocks to the castle. The castle protects the King while the King fights to protect his kingdom."

Jerry wanted to laugh, but her sincerity kept him from doing so. "You know, in the real world, the King doesn't fight for the kingdom; he sends his troops to fight for him."

"Quit splitting hairs, Jerry," Granny replied. She inhaled a deep breath into her lifeless lungs. "Feel the energy? It's calmer already. Let it work its magic to recharge you."

Granny was right. While at times it felt as if he were on a tilt-a-whirl, barely holding on by his fingertips, at the moment, the energy surrounding him felt welcoming. He turned, leaning against the Durango, enjoying the calmness of the moment.

"Did you really mean it?" Granny asked.

"It?"

"You told your friend you are a lucky man. I just wanted to know if you meant it."

He smiled. "I meant every word. I am a very lucky man."

"There was a time when you didn't feel that way."

He knew she was speaking of his lifelong struggle with what she referred to as the gift. He dug at the dirt driveway with the toe of his shoe. "It has its upsides."

"Which are?"

His smile morphed into a contented sigh. "It

brought me to April and Max."

"I'm glad you finally asked April to marry you. You two are good together. She'll be a good anchor for you."

"I hope she will be able to say the same."

"She already does. So does Max," Granny assured him.

Jerry looked over at the cleared lot, relieved not to see any of the spirits that he knew to still be near. "Looks like we'll be taking this sideshow a few miles up the road. I hope April and Max don't resent me for that. I know they both love me, but they've built a life here, and Max will be leaving her friends."

"Did Max show you her drawing?"

"Which one?"

"Of the house."

"She did."

"Then you know she's already seen the future there," Granny said. "Stop worrying, Jerry. It will be a good move; the other property is well-suited for the three of you."

"You could have warned me about this place," Jerry said without looking at her.

She laughed. "You're the psychic. You should have warned yourself."

"I've walked this property dozens of times. Never once did I feel anything amiss."

"That's because the spirits were settled. All will

be as it was once the dirt is replaced."

"It got a little heated out there. I'm surprised you didn't let me know you were there," Jerry said, circling back around to their previous conversation.

"I already told you. There was nothing I could do and nothing that ranger could have done either. Next time, just ask for help."

"I did ask for help."

"No, you were thinking of Tisdale."

"I'm not following you."

"Quit acting like a cop."

"Still not following."

"You're trying to control the situation and some things can't be controlled. They need to play out so you can help them find the solution. If you need help, ask for it. Asking for Gunter is expected. Other than that, leave the request open-ended. Why do you think some prayers don't ever get answered? It's because the person asking isn't asking for the right thing. Maybe they're not supposed to have that new car or be with the person who won't return their love. Think about it, if you'd have been able to find Holly's number sooner, you might have ended up with her instead of with April and Max. Remember that when you're on a job. Don't say who it is you need; just say I need help, and let the spirits figure out the rest."

Jerry chuckled.

"What's so funny?"

"You used to say I had a guardian angel looking over me, but I suddenly feel like a rockstar with a bunch of groupies."

"You are a rockstar. You always have been in my book. Some refer to the spirit as their guardian angel, as if there is only one. But we are both much smarter now. You can call them groupies if you want. Personally, I prefer spiritual entourage."

Gunter woofed.

Jerry looked to see Max running across the yard, wielding a shovel as if preparing to maneuver a canoe. Though Houdini could have easily outrun the girl, he checked his gait and remained at her side.

"Hey, Mr. Rockstar," Granny said. "The next time you start doubting yourself, I want you to remember that little girl there is your biggest fan."

"That admiration runs both ways, but thanks for the reminder," Jerry said. Pushing from the Durango, he ran to catch up with Max.

As he ran, Granny's words followed. "That's what I'm here for."

***

April and Carrie joined them as they finished covering the dirt. "So that's it?" Carrie asked, rubbing her arms.

Jerry looked out over the cleared lot. "For now. Max and I will finish marking the graves, and then I'll call in a landscaping crew to plant trees over each grave."

"I'm sorry," Carrie said softly.

Jerry knew she was referring to the fact that they wouldn't be building there. "It's alright, and don't worry, we will deed the property back to you."

Carrie shook her head. "No."

Jerry frowned. "I thought…"

"Carrie's afraid now that the property is cleared, he'll want to put up a pole barn," April said, answering for her.

Jerry knew Carrie's husband didn't believe in the gift, but it still came as a surprise he would violate the graves of those already buried on the land.

"He thinks we should call the council in Saginaw and have the bones removed," Carrie said without making eye contact.

"Did you tell him it wouldn't be a good idea to dig them up?"

"He's a good guy. He just can't wrap his mind around ghosts."

"Spirits," Max clarified.

"Me, I'm terrified. So, I'd rather keep them happy."

"Even if it means making your husband unhappy?" Jerry asked.

Carrie met his gaze. "I wouldn't be the one making him unhappy."

"Meaning you want us to keep the land in our name."

Carrie nodded. "I hate putting the responsibility

on you," she said softly.

"It became my responsibility the moment my dog dug up the grave," Jerry replied.

"I was wondering about that," Carrie said. "What would have happened if you weren't here to know the Indians were upset?"

"Max would have known," Jerry replied.

"No, I mean if neither you nor Max… Say someone dug them up but couldn't see the spirits to know they were angry."

"If the bones were treated well, then it is possible the spirits would settle down and accept their new resting place. But it is just as likely the spirits would linger near their original burying place and seek their revenge."

"By haunting the place?" Max asked.

"Perhaps, or it could come in a run of bad luck."

"They could really do that?" April asked.

Jerry could hear the unease in her voice. "Relax, Ladybug, not every spirit is malicious. Especially if they know the person responsible for disturbing their graves was just doing their job. Say, for instance, if Dan had been the one to unearth the body, only he didn't know because he scooped up a large pile of dirt and dumped it into a dump truck. While the chief would have been unhappy about it, he probably would have just followed the bones to their new location." Okay, so it was a stretch, but if it helped them sleep at night, so be it.

Carrie looked over the clearing. "How will you know where the others are buried?"

"The same way we found out about this one," Jerry said, nodding to the dogs.

"We owe Houdini a debt of gratitude," April replied in a babyish voice that she reserved exclusively for the puppy.

At the mention of his name, Houdini sidled up to April, wiggling his delight as the woman rewarded him with scratches.

Carrie laughed. "We need to work on your parenting skills. Children shouldn't get rewarded for misbehaving."

April shot a pointed look at her friend and smiled a sly smile. "He wouldn't have been misbehaving if the person watching him was doing their job."

"He wasn't misbehaving," Max said, jumping to Houdini's defense. "I trained him to look for bones. He was just doing his job." Max slapped her right leg, firming her chin when Houdini raced to her side without hesitation.

"He did it so well, we won't be living here." April studied her daughter as if choosing her words. "Max, you do know that means changing schools, don't you?"

"I know," Max said.

"You don't seem too broken up about the idea."

Max shrugged. "I've known it for a couple of weeks on account of the property didn't look right."

"I thought you drew the picture on the way from Frankenmuth," Jerry said, recalling the sketch.

"I did, but I'd seen it in my head before but didn't know what it meant."

"Sketch?" Carrie asked.

Max bobbed her head. "It's in my notebook." She retrieved the portfolio, bent the flap back, and turned it for all to see.

Though he and April had seen it before, the rendering was now finished and managed to catch them by surprise. April gasped as she traced the drawing, which now showed more detail.

"When did you finish that?" April asked.

"On the way home after we saw the property," Max replied.

"But you started it even before you saw the property, didn't you."

Max grinned. "Yep. I didn't know where it was, only that we weren't going to build here. Then, when you turned toward the airport, I felt the pull. When I saw the property, I knew."

"And yet, you still can't tell me the lottery numbers?" Carrie asked.

"No!" both Jerry and Max said at once.

***

Max sat on the couch staring at Houdini, who was crouched on the floor returning her stare. While Houdini had already received his K-9 Good Citizen Certification, Fred had now arranged for the trainer they'd been working with to use a training facility at Selfridge Air National Guard Base to administer the final round of testing to fully certify the dog as an official search and rescue dog. He further told her, once Houdini became a certified SAR dog working for the agency, Houdini would be permitted to travel with them wherever they went, as they never knew when they would be called into service.

She tilted her head and addressed the dog. "We've got three days left until your test. That means we have to up our training."

Houdini answered with a single high-pitched woof.

"No, I'm serious. This is going to be intense."

A loud bark filled the air.

Max turned to see Gunter standing over her. His presence surprised her, as she thought he'd gone with Jerry and her mom. She giggled and roughed his fur. "That's right, Gunter, you tell him."

Gunter lowered his head, making eye contact with Houdini, who answered with a loud bark that sounded much like that of his ghostly father.

That was the thing about Gunter being a ghost. Talking to him was almost like talking to a human. "You're such a good boy, Gunter. All I have to do is tell you something, and you do it." Max pondered that. *Houdini is part ghost, and everyone says how smart he is. Maybe it will work for him.*

"I knew you'd figure it out if I gave you time."

Max jumped and scrambled from the bed, staring at Gunter. Finally, she swallowed her shock. "When did you learn to talk?"

Laughter filled the room.

"If that dog gets to talk, then I get to come back to life."

Max scanned the room but saw no one. The fact that Gunter wasn't upset by the visitor kept her from screaming. She firmed her chin and tried not to show her fear. "Show yourself."

Instantly, a man appeared in front of her. Tall and thin, the spirit wore a white hat.

"Mr. Tisdale!" Max said confidently.

"At your service, ma'am."

"What are you doing here?"

"I came to see if you're finished with my rope."

Max eyed the rope they'd constructed into a harness for Houdini. "I thought you gave it to Jerry."

"I lent it to him," Tisdale corrected.

"Oh."

"Don't look so gobsmacked. It was only meant as a stopgap for an errant puppy. That boy's grown into a nice young dog."

"Houdini is great," Max agreed.

Tisdale arched his brow. "Why do I feel like there is a 'but' in there?"

"Because if he doesn't pass his training, he'll have to stay here whenever we're away. We can't count on him not to follow if we don't have the harness."

"I've been watching the two of you. He stays by your side when you walk and comes when called. I'd say he's pert near trained."

"I think so too, but Jerry said the trainer could have a trick or two up his sleeve and warned me not to underestimate him."

"Perhaps Jerry's trying to scare you so you don't skimp on the training," Tisdale mused.

"No, Jerry doesn't do that."

"No, I don't suppose he does. I guess that means you'd better keep up with the training. But I'm telling you that you're onto something with coming clean with the dog."

"Coming clean?"

"Telling the dog precisely what you expect," Tisdale clarified.

"Jerry said you didn't like dogs, so how come you seem to know so much about them?"

"No, I told him I didn't have any need for one. Dogs are fine with people who have a need for them."

"You think I have a need for one?"

Tisdale gave her a long look. "Can you shoot a gun?"

"I don't know. I never tried."

"I'll take that as a no. So that means you need a dog, and that dog should be with you wherever you go."

Max sighed. "Meaning you are going to take the harness."

Tisdale nodded. "Yes."

"But what if I need him to stay somewhere?"

"Then tell him. Now, don't go looking at me like that, little missy. I wouldn't be taking the rope if I thought you'd need it. You said it yourself: that pup is not an ordinary pup. If you want him to do something, then tell him. He has the capacity to understand you."

While Max wanted to believe him, she still had her doubts. "If he's so special, why did he chew the heel off Mom's favorite shoe?"

"Because at the end of the day, he's still a dog, and dogs need to chew on things," Tisdale said. He reached into his pocket and pulled out a ball.

While Gunter stood idly watching the show, Houdini's ears perked up as he swiped his mouth with his tongue.

Tisdale chuckled. "Yes, I see that got your attention, didn't it, boy?"

Houdini barked.

"Okay, here's the deal," Tisdale said, still staring at the dog. "This here ball is yours to keep. You want to chew on something, you chew on this. Understand?"

Another woof.

"Good," Tisdale said, handing the ball to Max.

Max rotated her hand to inspect the ball. "It looks

like it's made of leather."

Tisdale smiled. "Buffalo hide, mostly. There's a little something else in there to keep him satisfied. Secret ingredient—made it myself. I've got to be going, but you remember what I told you. Training is fine, but at the end of the day, you just think about what it is you want him to do, and he'll do it."

Max decided to test to see if it worked. *Houdini, down.*

Instantly, Houdini lowered to the floor, his eyes focusing on Max as if awaiting further instruction.

Houdini, roll over.

Once again, Houdini followed her silent instructions.

"It works." Max frowned. "What if someone else asks him to do something?"

Tisdale shook his head. "No need to worry yourself about that. He'll listen to Jerry and your mother. But he's attached to you."

"Attached?" She looked at Gunter. "You mean like Gunter is to Jerry?"

"Partly. The spirit part holds the attachment, but dogs are loyal. He knows you belong to him."

Max giggled. "That's a funny way of saying it."

"It's not funny. Animals know."

"How is it you know so much?"

Tisdale pushed his hat back with a finger. "I'm a Texas Ranger. It's our job to know."

Max scrunched up her face. "Really?"

"No, silly. It's because I'm dead. I am privy to all the good stuff." Tisdale winked. "That and the fact my horse, Laura Bell, was waiting for me on the other side. A glorious reunion that was, I guarantee. Listen, Ole Tisdale's got to go, but you quit fretting about that test. You just tell that pup what you expect. He won't let you down."

As soon as the spirit disappeared, Gunter faded out of view as well. She realized the ghostly K-9 had appeared only a moment before Tisdale. The knowledge was comforting. Though she no longer needed a babysitter, and Houdini had already shown himself to be capable of protecting her, she liked the fact Gunter still had her back.

Chapter Seven

Jerry paced the floor, feeling much like an expectant father waiting for news. Only the news he was waiting for was not of an impending birth but of whether Houdini passed his working dog qualification, which would allow him to travel with them wherever they went. While the trainer was impressed with the dog's ability to excel at any task, he'd made it clear that Houdini was young, and since he was slated to be an agency dog, he would not pass him if he weren't fully ready.

Jerry looked up just as Gunter stuck his head out the door. "Gunter, you're not thinking of breaking your promise to Max, are you?"

Gunter withdrew his head from the door and gave Jerry a sorrowful look.

"Stop pouting. I don't like it any more than you do."

Gunter yawned a squeaky yawn and looked at Jerry as if to say, *I know we promised, but the wait is excruciating.*

"Tell me about it, but a promise is a promise." Jerry pulled his cell from his pocket when the ring tone announced April's call. "Hello?"

"Hey," April's voice sang out. "How's it going?"

"I have no idea," Jerry said.

"What do you mean? Aren't you with them?"

"Nope. Sinclair didn't want any distractions during the initial testing, so he's only allowing one handler," Jerry said, speaking of the instructor Fred had sent to certify the dog.

"Can't you do your thing and tap into Max to see how it's going?"

Jerry chuckled. "I wish. I think I've worn a path in the tile."

"You've done it before," April reminded him.

"I'm not saying it's not possible. I'm saying I don't want to chance breaking their stride. If Houdini is following a command or following her silent commands, it could interrupt them. That happens at the wrong time, and the dog fails."

"Yeah, we don't want to chance that," April agreed. "Max is looking forward to Houdini coming with us on our trip. Besides, if he gets stuck, Gunter can help."

"Nope. Gunter is here with me."

Gunter tilted his head at the mention.

"Why? He's our ace in the hole."

"Max knows that, and it was her idea to keep him away. She's convinced Houdini is ready for whatever the instructor asks of him. She also knows he will have to stay with Carrie should he not pass his certification."

"I hope she's right."

"Relax, Ladybug. Max has been diligently working with him. She is confident in his abilities and is able to communicate with him the way I communicate with Gunter."

Gunter looked up once more, tilting his head so that his ears pointed to the wall.

"So, you're saying he has an unfair advantage?"

"I'm saying, between the two of them, this exercise will be a walk in the park. Besides, it's not like it's a competition where another dog won't get promoted."

"That's true," April agreed.

"What are you up to?"

"I've been at the computer since you left, trying to track down some information on Lina and Elke."

"How's it going?"

"Slow, but I'll get there."

"Fred said to let him know if you need any help."

"I've got this."

Jerry chuckled.

"What's so funny?"

"That's exactly what Max said when I asked if

she was sure she didn't want help."

"She is her mother's daughter," April agreed. "I think she also gets some of her stubbornness from you."

Jerry smiled, even though he knew her stubbornness to have been there well before he came into the picture. "You know, if you were to let Fred help, it would leave you more time to plan our wedding."

"Since Fred has so much spare time, maybe I should let him plan our wedding," April told him.

Jerry sucked in a breath. "Watch what you say."

April giggled. "What, you don't think Fred would make a good wedding planner?"

"I'm sure Fred would think he'd make a good wedding planner, but we both know he'd simply delegate it to someone else, which means you'd have to clear everything through the wedding planner. Now, I have no problem with that, but something tells me you'd prefer to have a bit more control over things."

"Yeah, you know me."

"I'd like to think I do." The truth of the matter was while April seemed pleased he'd finally gotten around to asking her to marry him, she'd not begun planning, nor had they settled on a date. Every time he'd brought it up, she changed the subject. While he knew something was bothering her, he didn't know what that something was. They were due to leave for Pennsylvania in two days, and the last thing he wanted was for the trip to be marred by whatever was troubling her. Preferring to bring it up when they could speak about it in person, Jerry made a mental note to talk to her about it when he returned home.

"Hey," she said, interrupting his thoughts. "I'm going to dive back into this. Have Max text me when she's done."

"Will do," Jerry promised. "Love you."

"Love you too."

The call had no sooner ended than his phone rang again, announcing Seltzer's call. Always happy to talk to his old boss, who'd not only been a mentor but, in some ways, felt more like a father than his own dad, Jerry smiled as he swiped to answer. "How are things in Pennsylvania?"

"Don't ask." Seltzer groaned.

"That bad?"

"Do yourself a favor and stay single."

While Jerry had intended to give him the news of his and April's engagement in person, he couldn't resist telling him now that he'd brought it up. "Too late for that piece of advice."

Instantly, Seltzer changed his tone. "Well, hot dang. You mean to tell me you finally summoned up the courage to ask April to marry you?"

Jerry's smile deepened. "I did."

"That's about the best news I've heard in ages."

"I thought you said…"

"Aww, don't mind this cranky old man. You know I adore June. I don't mind the being married part, I just hate the craziness leading up to it. June is so wired, you'd think Linda was her own daughter."

That Seltzer's wife had taken on a motherly role to the girl who he'd rescued alongside the road didn't come as a surprise. June was the proverbial mother hen and had looked after everyone in the station, including him. Jerry chuckled. "June has been a nurturer for as long as I've known her. I'm sure she is eating this up."

"June's got everything organized in this huge binder that is never too far away. She's using this experience to her advantage and is planning to turn it into a wedding planning guide for mothers of the bride. So, have the two of you set a date? I'm sure she won't mind printing things off for April when this wedding is over. Then again, she might just decide to visit you in Michigan and help April with the planning."

While Jerry loved June, April wasn't used to being smothered, and he wasn't sure she would be as thrilled as Linda to have her help. "No date yet. I think we are still getting used to being engaged."

"Take an old man's advice and elope. Doing so will go a long way to helping with the pre-wedding tension."

"I'll keep that in mind. April is looking forward to meeting June."

"Are you sure you won't stay with us?"

Jerry laughed. "June is stressed out enough as it is. We'll not add to it."

"Do me a favor. When she makes a fuss about you three staying in a hotel, perhaps you can just tell her you've gotten used to it. It seems reminding her she's stressed doesn't set too well."

Jerry laughed once more. "Sounds like you two need to take a vacation when this is all over."

"June's been trying to get me to go on a cruise. She seems to think her writing voices like the water."

"And you haven't gone? I seem to recall you like boats."

"I like fishing boats. I had my fill of ships when I was in the Navy. Then again, it might be fun to go on a ship where I don't have to work or stand watch."

"Sounds like the tide's already turning," Jerry said. "I'm sure you'll find some way to enjoy yourself while June's writing."

"Maybe you, April, and Max should come along." Seltzer's voice was serious.

While Jerry had never considered a cruise himself, the thought of taking April and Max on a cruise intrigued him. April had already said they'd never been anywhere before meeting him. He recalled how much he loved going topside when crossing the ocean with his unit. Devoid of surface light, the skies in the Mediterranean were the darkest he'd ever seen, with what looked to be a million stars twinkling for as far as one could see. Though they'd been headed into the war zone, those nights under the stars were ingrained in his memory. Jerry had felt the serenity, and the thought of sharing the experience with April and Max was nearly enough to get him to commit. *Don't do it, McNeal, at least not without asking April.* "It's tempting, but I'll have to ask April."

Seltzer emitted a hearty chuckle. "Haven't even made it official, and you're already wearing cuffs."

"You know, in all the years I've known you, I've never heard you so cynical about marriage. Are you sure you and June are okay?"

"June and I are fine. I'm just giving you a hard time. Listen, married life won't be all sunshine and roses. There will be a lot of give and take, but you find the right woman to share your life with, and there is nothing you won't do to make her happy."

"You mean like stepping aside while she plans weddings and going on a cruise when you'd rather go to your cabin and spend your time fishing?" Jerry asked.

"That's precisely what I mean." Seltzer laughed. "So, April's ex? What's his status?"

Jerry looked at Gunter, who was instrumental in thwarting Randy's planned revenge. "No longer a problem. There's enough camera footage and eyewitnesses to put him away for good this time,"

Jerry added.

"I still can't get over the fact that Gunter saved you."

"Again." Jerry glanced at Gunter, silently thanking him. "The dog saved us again."

"Have you ever wondered why he chose you and not Manning? I mean, if I had to choose, I'd pick you, but Manning was the dog's handler. So, why not him?"

They'd had this discussion before and could probably continue to contemplate it for many years to come. "Sarge, I don't know the why of it—perhaps I never will. All I know is my life hasn't been the same since he found me."

"I could say the same thing about you," Seltzer replied.

Jerry laughed.

"Now, come on, I'm being serious," Seltzer said.

"I know," Jerry said, "I'm just not used to you being so sappy."

"Just wait until you see me around the kid. That little bugger has me wrapped around his finger, and he hasn't even uttered his first word."

Seltzer was talking about Manning and Linda's son, Brian. Instantly, Jerry felt a pang of jealousy. It wasn't enough Seltzer and June had practically adopted Linda the moment Jerry had placed her in his old mentor's custody, but Linda had repaid them by naming her firstborn son after him. It wasn't that he objected to the arrangement, which seemed to be a good fit for everyone involved. But deep down, he'd thought it would be he who rewarded them with a grandchild. Jerry pushed the green-eyed monster aside. "I'm sure little Brian will be calling you Grandpa before you know it."

"Not Grandpa. I'm more of a Pappy or Papaw kind of guy."

Though the man couldn't see him, Jerry nodded his agreement. "I can see either of those working."

"Maybe we'll let Max decide since she's the oldest," Seltzer replied. "Gotcha. Listen, I know it has to sting a little, all this talk about Manning. I assure you, while he has his moments, that yahoo hasn't replaced you. He's still a couple of clowns short of a circus."

Jerry felt the heat of embarrassment in his cheeks. "And here, I thought I was the psychic."

"That wasn't me being a psychic. It was me being a dad."

"You're saying parents have a favorite?" Jerry asked.

"Nope. But if I did, it would be you. Hey, I hate to run, but I hear the kid squalling. I'd better see if June needs help."

"Okay, we'll see you soon."

"Looking forward to it," Seltzer said, ending the call.

Jerry had no sooner pocketed his phone than

Gunter barked and scrambled to his feet. Tail wagging, he stared at the door.

Max came in a moment later, her smile telling Jerry everything he needed to know.

Gunter greeted them both with a deep bark, and Houdini answered with an extravagant full-body wag.

"I gather things went well?" Jerry said, watching them.

Max bobbed her head. "Houdini did so good! He followed all my commands and found everything Mr. Sinclair had hidden, including his daughter, who was hiding in the back of a boat. It was crazy because he'd given me a sleeve to let Houdini smell and told me we were looking for the rest of the sweater. I could tell he was lying when he said it because I saw the girl's face in my mind and knew she was still wearing it. I knelt and allowed Houdini to smell it and told him who we were looking for. He took me right to her!"

Jerry could tell Max was holding something back. "You sound surprised. You've been working with him on this."

"Mr. Sinclair said he wanted to see just how good Houdini was. We spent five minutes training for a special search. Houdini passed that too!"

"What kind of search?"

Before she could answer, Sinclair came into the room. Dressed in khaki pants and a black sweatshirt, he was followed inside by a girl who looked to be around seven.

Sinclair nodded to Jerry, then beamed a smile at Houdini. "That's one smart dog you've got there, McNeal. The agency needs to find a way to clone him."

"He's her dog," Jerry said with a nod to Max, who grinned like a proud parent. "She deserves all the credit."

"All the same, I know good breeding when I see it, and that's some of the best I've seen."

Gunter woofed and smiled a K-9 smile.

"I tried to trick him up," Sinclare continued. "He excelled at everything, even things he hadn't been trained in."

"Like?" Jerry asked.

"Along with SARS, he'll be a certified K-9 forensics officer."

"That doesn't surprise me," Jerry replied. "He's already found several remains."

"We've included digital forensics," Sinclair clarified.

"He found two thumb drives and a hidden hard drive," Max said proudly. "We hadn't even practiced that. Mr. Sinclair just showed him what they use for training and only showed him once so he would know what he was looking for."

Jerry raised an eyebrow. "That's pretty impressive."

Sinclair took a call, and Max moved in to where only Jerry could hear. "I think that's why he did so good, because I showed him what we were looking for and told him what it was. We've practiced with remotes before, but I never thought of using a thumb drive."

Sinclair ended his call and pocketed his phone. "That was Mr. Jefferies. I gave him my report, which I'll file as soon as I get home." He turned to address Max and Houdini directly. "Sorry we couldn't have more of a ceremony, but Houdini is now part of the team and cross-certified for special operations. Good luck. I have no doubt you'll make the agency proud."

Max lowered to her knees and wrapped her arms around Houdini's neck. "Did you hear that, boy? You'll get to go everywhere with us, just like Gunter!"

"I wasn't aware you have another dog." Sinclar frowned. "If he's an agency dog, he'll have to be certified."

"Gunter's not with the agency. He's with me," Jerry clarified.

"You're with the agency. If the dog is with you, he'll still have to be certified," Sinclair said, standing firm. "Too bad you didn't bring him with you. I could have certified him today. Let me check my calendar," he said, pulling out his phone.

Jerry knew the man was going to run to Jefferies

the moment he left, and Fred would eventually tell the man why Gunter didn't need to be certified. He also knew Sinclair's daughter could see the dog. What he wasn't sure of was if it was because of her young age or because she, too, had the gift. He thought about reaching out to his grandmother but remembered what she'd said about keeping his requests open-ended. *If anyone is available, I could use a little help, please.*

Bunny appeared at his side, wearing a dress that closely matched her pink hair. "Bunny Emerson at your service. What can I do for you, Jerry?"

I think the little girl has the gift. She can see Gunter, so I wanted to see if she can see other spirits as well, Jerry said silently.

"You want me to scare her?" Bunny asked, raising her hands.

"No!"

Sinclair looked up from his phone. "What do you mean no? I haven't given you a date."

Jerry caught Max's attention. *Distract him for a moment, will you?*

Max nodded.

Just do something so we know if the girl can see you.

A second later, Bunny stood in front of him, face painted like a clown, juggling six lemons.

Emily giggled.

Jerry smiled. *I guess we've got our answer.*

Thanks for your help.

"Oh." Bunny's voice held a hint of disappointment as, one by one, she caught the lemons in the pocket of her dress. "And I was just getting started."

Of that, Jerry had no doubt. *Thanks for your help, Bunny.*

"Anytime," Bunny said, fading from view.

"Mr. Sinclair?" Jerry said, drawing the man's attention. "We won't be needing that appointment."

"But."

"No buts. The dog doesn't need to be certified because he's a ghost."

"You mean he works undercover?"

"I mean, he's a spirit. If you don't believe me, ask your daughter."

"My daughter? What does she have to do with this?"

"Nothing, except she can see spirits. Watch her hand," Jerry said, noting the fact the girl was scratching Gunter behind the ear.

"What's she doing?"

"Petting Gunter."

"The invisible dog?"

"He's not invisible. He's a spirit. Sometimes, seeing spirits runs in the family. Does anyone else in your family have the gift?"

Sinclair paled.

"You look a little green," Jerry told him. "Are

you feeling okay?"

"I'm good," Sinclair said. The man motioned for his daughter as he started for the door.

"He believed you," Max said the moment the door shut.

"I got the feeling there's something he's not telling us," Jerry agreed.

"I think he's got trouble," Max said, watching the door. "Maybe we should go after him."

"No, it's best to give him time to digest what I just said. He knows where to find us if and when he's ready to have a conversation."

"But..."

Jerry cut her off. "We can't force people to believe. I'll reach out to Fred and tell him it's okay to read the man in if he starts asking questions."

"What if he doesn't ask? You know how tough it can be on kids when people don't believe us."

Max had a point. "Okay, Max. I'll give the man a couple of weeks to come forward on his own. If we don't hear from him by the time we get back from Pennsylvania, I'll tell Fred about Emily."

Max laughed. "Why does Uncle Fred like people who have the gift so much?"

"That, my friend, is something I've been asking myself from the moment I met him."

"Maybe you should ask him."

Jerry chuckled. "Now, why didn't I think of that?"

Chapter Eight

"Jerry!" April's voice sang out from the dining room. "I found it."

Jerry knew she'd had a breakthrough in her search when he entered the room and saw Elke and Lina standing behind her, contentedly staring at the computer screen.

April turned the computer around so that he could see the Facebook profile of Nicole Krafft, a thin blonde woman who looked to be in her mid-thirties.

Jerry studied the photo of the woman, looking for any resemblance to either of the women. He saw none. "What's the relation?"

"She's married to Lina's great-grandson, Ben," April said, pulling the computer to her once more. "Ben's Facebook page is locked down, but Nicole is an open book."

"Meaning?"

April laughed and shook her head. "Meaning, she puts everything on there and would probably jump at the chance to tell the world about the keepsake."

Jerry looked at Lina and Elke. "Does she pass?"

April looked up from the screen. "I just told you she'd jump at the chance."

"I was asking them," Jerry said, nodding to where the spirits stood.

April smiled a sheepish smile. "Oh. And what are they saying?"

"Nothing yet, but I must say I'm very proud of you. You're a regular detective," Jerry said.

"I don't know about that. You did most of the work."

Jerry rocked back on his heels. "Me?"

"Yeah, you. I wouldn't have gotten anywhere with the keepsake alone, but since you were able to give me names, dates, and places, the trail was somewhat easy to follow. I'm telling you, we could take this show on the road and make a fortune from people researching their family tree. It would be much easier working backward than forward. I can see it now—we'd get a case and then just summon the spirit of the dead relative, who'd give us all the answers."

Jerry crossed his arms and shook his head. "Not

happening."

"Why?" April asked.

"Because you just described a séance."

"So?"

"Number one, they don't work, and number two, if they did, you'd be in for a lot of trouble."

"Why?" April asked once more.

"If a spirit wants to show themselves, that's one thing, but making a spirit appear just because you want something from them could fall back on you."

"You ask for help from spirits all the time," April reminded him.

"The key to that sentence is, I ask. I don't use magic and crystal balls to summon them. Just like the living, spirits have free will. Summon them against their wishes, and you'll be asking for trouble."

April closed her laptop. "You're contradicting yourself. You just said séances don't work; now you are saying it's terrible to summon spirits against their will."

"Séances don't work because they are not needed and are usually performed by people who are only in it for profit."

"Savannah gets paid to tell fortunes. What's the difference?"

"Mostly because Savannah isn't a fraud. When she gives readings, she is actually communicating with the spirit. That's not always the case. There are plenty of people out there just looking to prey on people's grief. It's been going on since the beginning of time."

"I remember reading that Harry Houdini spent thousands trying to contact his mother after her death," April said.

"Yes, and calling psychics out for being frauds," Jerry agreed.

"Too bad he couldn't have met someone like you." April beamed.

"He may have called me a fraud too," Jerry surmised.

"But you can see spirits."

"I can see spirits who wish to be seen. Just because a person asks to contact someone who is no longer with us doesn't mean that spirit is reachable."

"Why not?"

"Sorry, Ladybug. I'm afraid I do not have all the answers. No one does. Anyone who claims to is lying."

"I like him. Maybe we should stay," Lina said. "Her too. She's rusty, but with a little work, she'll come around."

He'd been so involved in the conversation, he'd totally forgotten they were there.

"He's honest," Elke agreed. "But they aren't family, and we need to be with family."

"So where in Michigan does the great-grandson live?" Jerry said, hoping it would be close enough to drop the heirloom off before leaving for Pennsylvania.

April grinned. "That's the best part. They live in Pennsylvania."

Okay, this was a pleasant surprise. "Seriously? What part?"

"DuBois. I was just getting ready to look to see where it was in relation to Chambersburg." April lifted the cover of the laptop and typed the town into Google Maps.

"Oh, Max is going to love this," Jerry said. He placed his fingers on the touchscreen and expanded the view to show the town of Punxsutawney, Pennsylvania.

"That's where they filmed the movie *Ground Hog Day*!" April said excitedly.

"Hate to burst your bubble, but it was actually filmed in Illinois," Jerry said.

"Oh. I thought it was a real town."

"It's real with all the fanfare and where they host the Groundhog Festival each year at Gobbler's Knob. You just won't find some of the houses and locations if you go looking for them. Gobbler's Knob is up on the mountain and not in the city square."

"You've been there?"

Jerry nodded. "I volunteered for assignment during the festival during my first year as a trooper."

"You don't sound too happy about that. Didn't

you have fun?"

"They start running buses up to Gobbler's Knob at three am. From then until around nine am, it is a standing-room-only event with booze and bands. Most of the visitors behave, but there are always a few that overindulge. The town square is abuzz from dawn with vendors selling beer and barbeque."

April frowned. "I always thought it was a family event."

"It is family-friendly. It's well organized, and the town's folks are gracious hosts. You can catch the movie *Groundhog Day* at the Community Center, see Phil sleeping off the excitement in his den after his performance and shop at one of the stores in town."

April scrunched up her face. "So why didn't you have fun?"

"Because I was working." Jerry winked.

April smiled a knowing smile. "When you'd rather be playing."

"That, and the crowds."

"We don't have to go."

"Oh, we're going, especially since we'll be so close. There'll be tourists, but nothing like the February crowd. Besides, the whole town is filled with groundhog statues, and there will be plenty of chances for photo ops."

April closed the computer once more. "I'm so looking forward to this vacation. It's going to be perfect!"

Gunter yawned.

"Uh oh," Lina said.

"Indeed," Elke agreed.

Jerry ran his hand over the back of his neck.

"What's wrong?" April asked.

While Jerry wanted to tell April the consensus of those in the room thought she'd just jinxed the trip, he kept that information to himself. "Nothing's wrong," he said instead.

"You rubbed your neck. You always do that whenever you're worried or upset."

"Or when I've been bending over the computer," he said, rolling his neck to emphasize his point.

April studied him as if trying to see the validity of his statement. "Okay, but we promised not to keep any secrets from each other."

"We're going on vacation, and we're going to have fun." Jerry bent and kissed her on top of her head as if sealing the deal.

***

Jerry pressed the gas pedal, silently thanking Fred for helping him navigate driving a full arsenal across Canada and easily crossing back to American soil.

"You look happy," April said from the passenger seat.

Jerry glanced in her direction. "I'm always

happy."

"Not always. But you don't just look happy. You look really happy."

Jerry reached for April's hand and kissed her engagement ring. "I'm pretty sure I'm supposed to be happy at this stage in my life."

"I'm happy too. I know I'm not psychic, but I feel there's something different today," April told him. "Is it because we're heading to Pennsylvania?"

That, and the fact we were able to pass through the border without getting arrested, Jerry thought to himself. "Traveling with you is fun. But, yes, this trip has a bit of a homecoming feel to it. I'm looking forward to seeing everyone."

"We don't have to build in Michigan, you know," April said without conviction.

"Are you forgetting that we just bought six lots that are being cleared even as we speak?"

"I just want you to be happy." This time, her words rang true.

"I'm happy. I am also excited to be on a road trip with my family." He looked in the mirror. Max sat in the middle row, wearing her headphones. Her eyes were closed, as were Houdini's, who lay in the seat beside her with his head in her lap. Aside from the fact that Gunter sat beside them with his head hanging out the closed window and the entourage of spirits in the backseat, they could pass for a normal family of three heading out to explore the world. He decided to take a chance. "Speaking of family. Have you given any more thought to setting a date?"

"Nothing definitive. You know I've been caught up in tracking down Elke and Lina's family."

It was the same excuse she'd used every time he'd broached the subject. It wasn't being with him that held her back, of that he was certain, but she'd yet to tell him the real reason. "You're not getting cold feet, are you?" He knew the answer but was hoping it would get her talking.

"Not about you."

"But?"

"It's the whole wedding thing I'm having trouble with."

"I'm not following you."

"Weddings cost a fortune."

Jerry laughed and caught himself keeping the humor from his voice as he spoke. "You're worried about money?"

"Just because we are set financially doesn't mean we have to throw it away on a wedding that no one comes to."

Now, we're getting somewhere. "What do you mean no one comes to? We have lots of friends."

"They're your friends, Jerry." April held up a hand. "It's true. With the exception of Carrie, everyone we would invite to the wedding were your friends first. Even the spirits are here because of you."

Jerry checked the mirror and saw Lina, Elke, and Bunny watching. Though he didn't see her, he knew his grandmother's spirit was hovering close. He took the exit for the welcome center, found a parking place, and turned off the Durango.

"Are you coming in, Mom?" Max said, taking off her headphones and hooking on Houdini's leash.

"I probably shouldn't let her go in alone," April said, unfastening her seatbelt.

"She's not going in alone." Jerry looked in the mirror once more. "Everyone out. You too, Gunter. April and I want to talk, so I want all of you to stay with Max."

They all got out. Jerry took April's hand in his and started in the opposite direction of the welcome center. "Okay, spill it," he said once they'd walked a short distance.

"It's the wedding planner," April said without looking at him.

Since they hadn't actually hired a wedding planner, he knew she was talking about the book Seltzer's wife had sent. "June's great at planning things. If you have a question, I'm sure she could help you out."

"I have nothing but questions," April said. "Maybe we should just…"

Jerry stopped. "Are you breaking up with me?"

"No, of course not," she said and began walking once more. "I just don't need a big, extravagant wedding to make me feel married. Heck, I already feel like we're married. Can't that be enough?"

"No."

"You mean you want a big wedding?"

"No," Jerry repeated.

"So, you want to elope?"

"No, not unless you do."

April emitted a nervous giggle. "You're not helping."

"I don't need a big wedding, but I want you to be my wife. If not for us, then for Max. She needs to know I belong here."

"She knows," April told him. "We already know you're committed to us. You don't have to prove anything."

"Maybe not, but I blew it on the proposal, so I think our wedding should feel special."

"You didn't blow it."

"Now, about the wedding," he said, circling around.

"So, you do want a big wedding?"

"That's not what I said. I just want a little more than standing in front of strangers and saying 'I do.'"

"What do you suggest?" April asked.

"Let me work on it," Jerry said.

"Maybe we should figure it out together," April suggested.

Jerry cocked an eyebrow. "You don't trust me?"

April giggled.

Jerry pretended to take offense. "I'll have you know I'm full of good ideas."

"Just promise to tell me if you plan on wearing a disguise," April said, biting her lip.

Instantly, Jerry recalled the fumbled proposal when he'd donned the Santa suit. "Who told you?"

"No one told me. I pieced everything together, and Max confirmed. I'm sorry I took that away from you."

Jerry shrugged. "At least I was fast enough to duck the blow. I'd hate to have had to explain the black eye. I'd have had to start calling you Slugger instead of Ladybug."

"Maybe it would be safer if we brainstorm things together," April offered.

"I'd like that," Jerry said, pulling her into his arms.

Chapter Nine

Jerry, April, Max, Houdini, and their spirit entourage stood at the foot of the hill, looking up at the stately two-story white siding house on E. Long Avenue.

"Maybe you should go in alone," April said, clutching the frame.

"Where's your sense of adventure?" Jerry asked.

April laughed a nervous laugh. "This isn't about adventure. It's about not coming across as kooks. I still say we should have contacted Nicole and Ben ahead of time so they would know we were coming."

"Then we couldn't have seen their faces when you showed them our heirloom." Elke's statement sent a cool breeze through the air.

April turned away from the house. "Okay, I felt that. Which one did I make mad?"

"Good catch. Elke was just reminding us we'd agreed to do this in person so she could judge the couple's sincerity if they agreed to take the keepsake," Jerry said, explaining the breeze.

"I've learned from the best," April said. "So now what? We just knock on the door?"

"That's one way to see if they're home," Jerry said.

Houdini leaned forward. His nose quivering, he gave a sorrowful whine as Gunter pushed through the closed door.

Max lowered her hand, flattening her palm in front of the dog's face, reminding the young shepherd to stay. Houdini stayed put but remained focused on the front door.

April raised an eyebrow. "You said that was one way. What's the other way?"

Jerry smiled. "Gunter just went in to check things out. We'll know shortly."

"What if they aren't home?" April asked.

Jerry looked at the house and saw Gunter sticking his head out the front door as if waiting for them to join. "They're home."

April lifted the frame and started up the hill. "Good, I figured with the luck we've been having of late, they would be on vacation or something."

"Here, let me carry that for you," Jerry said, taking the frame from her and motioning her forward. "You found them; you take the lead."

April walked up the concrete steps in determined strides, rapping on the storm door even before he and Max reached the porch.

The inner door opened. Not appearing overly friendly, Nicole Krafft stared out through the glass while pointing to the 'no soliciting' sign taped to the door. So much for the woman being an open book, as Jerry didn't recall seeing the noticeable pregnancy bump in any of the Facebook photos April had shown.

"We're not selling anything," April said.

Nicole closed the door without responding.

"Well, that was just out and out rude," Lina said.

"Indeed," Elke said and walked through the closed door.

Bunny looked at Jerry. "I guess they are loners."

"It's a good thing the sisters aren't vampires," Jerry said, watching Lina follow Elke inside.

Max snickered.

April frowned. "What did I miss?"

"Elke and Lina went inside. If they were vampires, they would have had to wait to be invited," Jerry said.

April stared at him without blinking.

"What?"

"You're telling me vampires are real?" April said, finding her voice.

Jerry laughed. "I sure hope not. I have enough to deal with without worrying about the undead."

"But you said."

"Elke and Lina went in without being invited. I merely said if they were vampires, they couldn't have entered."

"Good one, Jerry," Bunny said.

Jerry used his thumb to ease the worry line between April's brows. "It was a joke, Ladybug. As far as I know, there are no such things as vampires."

"Uh huh, and before I met you, there were no such things as ghosts," April mumbled.

Jerry winked. "Oh, they were here; you just didn't know about them."

"Exactly. So, who's to say there aren't any vampires?" April asked.

"She's got a point, Jer," Bunny told him. "Take it from me, I didn't believe in spirits until I became one."

Max snickered.

Jerry placed the frame on the ground between his legs and used his hands to turn April back toward the door. "Go forth and conquer."

April sighed. "Maybe you should give it a try. They don't like me."

"My fiancée is no quitter. Now raise your hand and knock on that door like you mean business," Jerry said firmly.

April doubled her fist and pounded on the storm door.

Houdini barked his encouragement.

Nicole opened the inside door. "We already belong to a church, and I don't want to discuss politics." She lifted her cell phone for them to see. "Go away, or I'll call the police."

"I knew I should have e-mailed her," April said over her shoulder.

"It's harder than it looks," Jerry agreed. "The good news is she hasn't already made the call. It shows her to be more cautious than hateful. Tell her what you want before she closes the door again. You might not get another chance."

April pulled herself taller. "Please, we're here to talk to Ben."

Nicole looked her over. "What do you want with MY husband?"

"I have something that belongs to him," April replied.

This time, Nicole's gaze trailed to Max, who'd yet to utter a word.

"Oh, for Pete's sake," Jerry held the frame up for the woman to see and whispered to April. "Want me to show her my badge?"

April shook her head. "Let me give it one more try. Nicole…Mrs. Krafft? Please, my name is April Buchanan. My family and I drove all the way from Michigan to talk to your husband about his third great-grandmother. I promise all we want is a couple moments of his time."

Nicole held firm to the door and called over her

shoulder, "Ben, they want to talk to you about your great-grandmother."

"Third." April's words fell on deaf ears as Nicole moved aside and Ben stepped up to the door.

Wearing red flannel and jeans, he peered through the storm door, oblivious to the fact that Gunter was standing beside him.

Jerry held up the frame for him to see.

Ben's gaze took in the frame. "I've never seen that before."

"It belonged to Lina Krafft. She was your third great-grandmother. We bought it at an auction and traced it to you."

The tension in the man's face eased. "You got proof?"

April nodded and pulled a piece of paper from her pocket. While the paper wasn't authentic, the words written on it were and showed a direct lineage from Ben Krafft to Lina Krafft. It was April's idea—and she and Jerry had worked on it together. At April's insistence, they'd also stopped at an antique store where they'd purchased a weathered notebook and used one of the faded pages to detail the history behind the display. April handed the paper to Ben, who looked it over and opened the door.

He stepped aside to allow them entrance. "Please come in. Sorry for the mistrust. We used to live in the city, and you never know who's knocking at your door."

"Smart man," Jerry agreed as they followed him to what looked like the main living room.

"Jerry used to be a Pennsylvania state trooper," Max said proudly. "Now he lives in Michigan with me and Mom."

"There's a nursery with two cribs, but I don't see any other children," Elke said as she and Lina appeared beside the man.

"DuBois looks like a nice place to raise a family," Jerry said casually.

"I hope so." Ben motioned them to the couch. "That's why we moved here. Nicole is pregnant, and neither of us want to raise our children in the city."

"Twins!" Max blurted. "I knew it."

Nicole had just stepped into the room carrying a bowl of water. Her face paled. "Do I look that big already?"

While Jerry had also picked up on the news, he'd hoped to keep the fact they were psychics under wraps since the couple were already on alert. *Easy, Max, we don't want to freak them out,* Jerry said without speaking.

Nicole held the bowl out. "Your dog looks thirsty. Can he have some water?"

Jerry nodded. "Of course, thank you."

Nicole bent and sat the bowl on the floor in front of Houdini, who eagerly lapped at the contents.

"You don't look fat at all," Max said. "He said children, so I just guessed."

"It was a good guess," Ben said proudly. "Two boys. I can't think of a better Christmas present."

"Boys!" Lina said, clasping her hands together. "That means there will be more heirs to keep watch over our mother's things."

"Indeed," Elke agreed. "One for each of us to spoil!"

"So tell me about this," Ben said, peering at the frame.

April handed him the newly created history of the piece.

Ben read the paper and handed it to his wife. "I can't wait to show my students."

"Ben's a history teacher," Nicole explained.

Jerry smiled inwardly at seeing Elke's shoulders relax. Someone interested in history would be an unlikely candidate for tossing the heirloom aside.

"I'm surprised the paper stayed with the frame," Ben said, running his fingers across the glass.

"It was in the glass," April said. She frowned when Nicole snickered.

Nicole waved her off. "Sorry, it's a line from the television show *Justified.* The woman keeps poisoning people, and when questioned as to how, she tells them it was already in the glass."

April nodded her understanding before continuing. "I hope you don't mind that I changed out the frame. It was in poor condition and not original to the piece."

"Why change out the frame if you weren't going to keep it?" Nicole asked.

April's eyes went wide, then recovered. "We were going to keep it at first. That's why we bought it. Then I discovered the history of the piece and knew I had to try and find the family."

As April wove the lie, Jerry noticed that her face turned the cutest shade of pink.

Gunter growled. Houdini alerted, and the hairs on the back of Jerry's neck stood on end. A second later, heavy footsteps sounded overhead. Only instead of being in unison, the steps sounded oddly off.

"Jerry?" Max's voice echoed her fear.

"I told you the house is haunted," Nicole blurted. She slid closer to her husband, watching Houdini, who now faced the stairway, mimicking his father's menacing growls.

April glanced at the ceiling. "You mean there's no one up there?"

Nicole shook her head.

"Everywhere we go," April said and burst out laughing.

"It's not funny," Ben said, clutching his wife's hand. "We've only been in the house three months. What are we supposed to say when we put the house on the market so soon?"

"That we're selling the house because it's haunted," Nicole said. "I tried to get him to call an exorcist, but Ben said it would only draw attention to the house and make it harder to sell."

Elke stood and walked to the stairs. "Sister and I were just up there. We didn't see anyone, living or dead."

Gunter barked, skirted around Elke, and raced up the stairs when the footsteps sounded once more.

"Maybe we should go take a look around," Elke said.

Bunny took hold of her arm. "The man said the place is haunted."

Elke pulled her arm free and looked in Jerry's direction. "Tell me she's kidding."

Houdini woofed then looked at Max as if asking permission.

"Houdini, stay," Max said.

"Let him go," Ben said. "Maybe he'll scare off the ghost."

Jerry nodded when Max looked to him for direction.

"Houdini, break," Max unhooked the leash, and the young dog raced up the stairs.

All eyes turned to the ceiling, listening as Houdini raced back and forward overhead. Several moments later, both dogs returned. Houdini plopped on the floor, watching the stairs.

Ben eyed Houdini. "I don't suppose I could convince you to sell that dog?"

"He's not for sale," Jerry said. "But perhaps I

could be of service."

Nicole narrowed her eyes. "I told you they were up to something."

"The only thing we are up to is bringing you this collection and telling you of the history that surrounds it," Jerry said. "I offered to help with your spirit problem because it's what I do."

"What is what you do?" Ben asked.

"He's a ghostbuster," Bunny said. "Though I'm not even sure that's a thing, on account of he doesn't really bust anything. Jerry, what is it you do again?"

Jerry ignored the wayward spirit and focused on the couple. "I'm a Paranormal Investigator."

"You're a ghostbuster?" Nicole said.

Bunny beamed a smile. "See, I told you."

Jerry shook his head. "I'm not a ghostbuster."

"Do you hunt ghosts?" Nicole asked.

"Mostly, they hunt him." April snickered.

"You're not helping," Jerry told her.

"Do you see any ghosts here with us?" Nicole asked.

Jerry made it a point to look around the room. "Nope." Technically, it wasn't a lie, as Granny had told him entities preferred to be called spirits.

"Liar, liar, pants on fire," Bunny said, waving her arms.

Bunny, go wait outside before I make you stay here when we go, Jerry said without speaking.

"You're not leaving her here with us!" Elke said.

"Make me how?" Bunny asked.

Gunter growled.

"Oh, poo," Bunny said, then disappeared.

Jerry stood and pulled out his badge. "Listen, you don't have to believe me, but I'm pretty good at what I do. If you want me to check it out, I will. If not, we will be on our way."

"It'd be cheaper than an exorcism," Ben said to his wife. "It's your call, honey."

She ran a hand over her baby bump. "I really want to raise our boys in this house."

Jerry looked at April. "I'll take Max with me. It's your call, but I'd prefer you stay down here with Nicole."

"How come the kid can watch and I can't?" Nicole asked.

"Max can see spirits, and you're pregnant. Listen, I know it sounds exciting and all, but it will mostly be you standing there watching me talk to myself."

Ben arched an eyebrow. "You talk to yourself?"

Sometimes. Jerry kept that thought to himself. "No, but unless you can see spirits, it will look like I'm talking to myself. You don't have to be quiet, but if you ask questions about what's going on, then it makes it a lot harder for me to do what I need to do."

"Which is?" Nicole asked.

"Find out who is haunting your house." Jerry looked at Ben. "How about you? Think you can be quiet and let me do my job?"

Ben didn't look all that excited to go upstairs, but he nodded his agreement.

Even before they reached the second floor, Jerry knew that whoever had made the noise was gone. He looked to Max for confirmation.

"Houdini must have scared them away," Max said, leaving out Gunter's involvement.

"You mean the ghost is gone?" Ben's tone showed his relief.

"For now," Jerry told him.

Ben's shoulders slumped. "You mean it will be back?"

Unwilling to give the man false hope, Jerry nodded. "My guess is the dog scared the spirit away. It might be an hour, a day, a week, or longer, but I'd lay odds it will return unless we can find out why it is here."

"So you're saying we need to get a dog?"

"You could, but I'm not saying that would be a permanent fix. It's best to fix the problem."

Ben rocked back on his heels. "Uh-huh. And just how much is that going to cost?"

"Nothing."

"We both know there's nothing free in the world, Mr. Buchanan."

Buchanan? Jerry retraced the conversations and realized that April had given her last name and had only introduced him and Max by first name.

"McNeal. April is my fiancée. To answer your question, there is no charge. I work for the government, and this is what I do."

Ben blew out a whistle. "I knew the government likes to throw around money, but I didn't know they employ ghostbusters."

Jerry ignored the quip and focused on a shelving unit that seemed to have captured the dog's attention. Sitting in the nursery, the shelf had slanted shelves that boasted a fresh coat of bright white paint. "What's the story behind this shelf?"

"Story?"

"How long have you had it, and where'd you get it?"

"Got it a couple weeks ago. Bought it at the antique store here in town. Nicole and I are voracious readers. We want to instill our love for books in the boys. So we thought it would be a good way to display books for them. See how the shelves are slanted? This way, the boys will be able to see the covers instead of the spines."

Gunter sat staring at the shelf as Houdini whined and pawed at the bottom.

Ben eyed the dog. "You're saying the shelf is haunted?"

Probably. Jerry decided to keep that to himself for the time being. "I'm saying I would like to do some digging into the history of the shelf. That antique shop? Is it open today?"

Ben bobbed his head. "Yep, the Junk Dealer's Daughter. It's only a couple blocks from here. Want me to go with you?"

"No. I think you should stay here with your wife." Jerry reached into his wallet and handed him a business card. "We'll go have a talk with the owner and then come back and let you know what we find out."

"Darius."

"Excuse me?"

"He's the fellow who owns the place. Just look for a young guy in glasses with sideburns. He's a super nice guy and strikes a fair deal."

Jerry paused at the top of the stairs. "There's no need to further upset your wife. I think it best not to mention the bookshelf just yet."

Ben didn't look convinced. "She'll ask what you found."

"Yep, and you'll tell her that the entity was gone by the time we got upstairs," Jerry replied.

"Think she'll believe us?"

Jerry smiled. "Why wouldn't she? It's the truth."

***

"What exactly happened in there?" April asked once they were seated in the Durango.

"It's just like Ben said. The spirit was gone by the time we got upstairs."

"No, I'm talking about before you even went up. I know you can talk to spirits with your mind, but I admit I was getting a little worried because even though you were talking to Ben, it looked as if you were fighting demons."

Jerry recalled the conversation with Bunny. "Have you ever seen any old Bugs Bunny cartoons where Elmer Fudd is hunting the rabbit?"

April knitted her brows. "Bugs Bunny was a bit before my time, but I've seen a few."

Jerry looked in the mirror and focused on the pink-haired lady as he spoke. "It was kind of like that."

Bunny stared him down. "I hate to tell you this, Jerry, but the rabbit always won."

Chapter Ten

True to Ben's words, it took longer to walk down the hill in front of the house and get into the Durango than to actually drive to the Junk Dealer's Daughter. Finding no available parking on the street, Jerry circled the block and parked in the public lot. He noted the mural for Luigi's Ristorante on the maze-colored building that flanked the parking lot—a simple scene that showed an Italian couple speaking to each other through open windows. The woman had a red wrap draped around her shoulders, with a bottle of wine sitting on the table next to her. The gentleman wore a white apron over an equally white shirt and had a glass of red wine sitting on the windowsill in front of him. His age spoke of a man who'd witnessed a lot over the years. He looked to be in no hurry to return to the heat of the kitchen as he leaned out the painted window and appeared to be hanging on the woman's every word. As he put his card in the parking meter, Jerry smiled. "Anyone up for Italian food before we leave town?"

"I'm in," Max said.

"I could go for some spaghetti and meatballs," April said, glancing at the mural. "I also plan on sticking my head in the candy store. Do you want me to wait until after we go to the antique store?"

"No, you go ahead. It will give me a chance to see if I pick up on anything on my own. Max, you and Houdini can go with your mom if you'd like. I'll take Gunter with me." While he'd expected her to argue, Max readily agreed to go with her mother, leaving him to wonder if she was still uneasy about going to places with so much energy from the past. He started to ask, but she seemed genuinely eager to explore the candy shop. Jerry left them to it and crossed the road, his eyes trailing over the three-story cream-colored building. The Junk Dealer's Daughter took up the right side of the combined building. While the store to the left had a black awning stretched across the front, the Junk Dealer's Daughter had a simple black sign with the store's name showcased in white lowercase letters—a lovely, unintrusive welcome to all who entered.

The entry to the building transitioned to a brick walkway flanked by glass window displays. The main door sat back about six feet from the sidewalk.

Jerry stopped to check out the window displays, which housed an antique table and chair on the left and a static display of antique Americana items on the right. Gunter moved ahead of him, sniffing the area around the glass.

Jerry stepped into the vestibule. As his foot made contact with the brick, Gunter growled a profound warning. Jerry blinked, watching as the displays changed before his eyes, morphing into a display of men's and women's shoes. While the styles looked dated, the shoes themselves appeared to be brand new.

The door opened, and an older woman in a pale pink blouse and gray herringbone skirt that fell just below her knees waved him inside. As she moved back, her high-heel pumps clicked on the tile floor. "Come, Mr. McNeal, we've been waiting for you."

That the spirits knew he was coming didn't surprise him. Jerry entered the building, surprised to see a host of shoes lining not only the walls but also displayed on top of the waist-high counters, which lined a staircase in the center of the vast room. Several people milled about the room in various stages of picking out or trying on shoes. Jerry heard footsteps, much like the ones he'd heard in the house a few moments before.

He turned toward the noise and saw a man with a peg leg. The guy hobbled back and forth in the aisle, trying out the fit of a single shoe on his right foot. The fellow looked up, saw Jerry watching, and smiled a sly smile.

Instantly, Jerry knew he was the spirit haunting Ben and Nicole's house. He started toward the entity, hoping to ask the spirit some questions. The spirit bolted, his peg thumping along the tile floor as he ran around the stack of shoes, then clumped his way down the stairs.

Gunter, I need to talk to that man, Jerry said without speaking.

Gunter woofed, then took off after the errant soul.

Jerry started for the stairs, intending to follow.

"Hello?"

Jerry experienced a wave of dizziness as the stairs disappeared and the rest of the room morphed into their current state. The rich walls of the past were now a light beige that blended with the square-tiled drop ceiling. Several beams ran horizontally across the ceiling, painted the same mint green as the trim along the doorframe. The slanted shelves, which had been there seconds earlier, were now replaced with an array of antiques, leaving the room full without seeming overly cluttered. Jerry turned toward the voice and saw a man who looked to be close to him in age. Ben had been right about the sideburns, which curved along the jawline and neared his chin.

Dressed in khaki pants, a black T-shirt, and a

beanie cap, Darius eyed him cautiously. "Are you all right there, buddy? You look as if you've seen a ghost."

I've seen one or two in my lifetime, Jerry said silently. Jerry realized that, in his haste, he'd forgotten to protect himself and wondered how long the man had been watching. "I didn't see you standing there," Jerry said truthfully.

"I just got here. I was in the basement and didn't hear you come in. Normally, I listen for footsteps."

Jerry recalled the man with one shoe. "Ever hear any that aren't here?"

"Is that your way of asking if the place is haunted?" Darius asked.

"Just making conversation," Jerry replied. "You said this building has a basement?"

"I did." The man rounded the counter and sat on a tall stool.

Jerry tapped at the floor with the toe of his shoe. "My guess is the stairs would have been right about here."

Darius looked over the counter as if to see what had given the location away. "Good guess."

"It wouldn't happen to have been a shoe store at one point, was it?" Jerry asked, knowing the answer.

The man sat back on the stool and crossed his arms. "Either you're an excellent guesser, or you know more about this building than you're letting on."

Jerry searched the man's face, wondering what his reaction would be if he were to tell him the truth, then decided to try a soft approach. "You sold Ben and Nicole Krafft a shelf a few weeks back."

The man chuckled and reached a hand over the counter. "Darius Clement. Any friend of Ben's is a friend of mine. You had me going for a moment. I should have known someone had told you about the basement."

"Jerry McNeal," Jerry said, shaking the man's hand. He let go. "Ben and I aren't friends. He told me about the shelf but didn't mention the basement."

Darius cocked an eyebrow. "You're not friends, but you know him. He told you about the shelf but not the basement. Why do I have the feeling I'm missing a piece of the puzzle?"

"Because you are." Deciding there was no easy way, Jerry dove into it. "My family and I came here to return an artifact that had been in Ben's family for over a hundred years. While there, we heard footsteps upstairs. Long story short, that shelf has a spirit attached to it."

Darius laughed. "You're kidding, right?"

Jerry stood firm. "I never kid about spirits."

The smile evaporated. "Say I was to believe you. Ben and Nicole have only been in the area for a couple of months. How do you know it's the shelf that's haunted and not the house?"

Jerry blew out a sigh. "Because I followed the

spirit here and watched him. I also watched my dog disappear down those stairs no one can see."

"I just came from the basement. I didn't see any dog." To his credit, Darius sounded more amazed than skeptical.

Jerry nodded. "That's because my dog is also a spirit."

Darius glanced at the phone sitting on the counter.

Hoping to avoid explaining himself to the local police, Jerry flashed his badge and handed Darius his business card. "I'm not crazy. I'm psychic."

Darius studied the card. "Lead paranormal investigator for the Department of Defense. That's a thing?"

Jerry nodded.

"How does one get that job?"

It was Jerry's turn to laugh. "Just lucky, I guess."

"So, what, you're some kind of ghostbuster or something?"

Tired of arguing, Jerry shook his head. "Something like that, and before you ask, I don't lock the spirits in canisters."

"Why not?"

"Because there aren't enough canisters in the world to contain them all."

Darius blew out a whistle. "That many, huh?"

"Yep."

"So, what's the plan? You do have a plan, don't

you?"

"Most of the time, it's as simple as talking to the spirit. Sometimes, they know what they are doing is causing problems, and sometimes, they don't have a clue. On occasion, the spirit doesn't know they are dead, so it's just a matter of letting them know."

"This ghost you're looking for, is he here now?"

While there'd been more when he'd had his vision, only two remained in the room: a young woman and the elderly woman who had welcomed him inside. The one he was looking for had not returned. "He's not here."

Darius frowned his disappointment. "You know, I didn't want to say anything because I thought you were a kook, but I may have felt a thing or two."

Jerry was intrigued. "Like?"

"A cold spot or a shadow." He smiled. "Got to watch who you tell that to, you know."

Jerry nodded his understanding as he looked about the room. His gaze settled on a cream-colored curio cabinet that sat in a crook on the opposite side of the room. The woman had a rag in her hand, ignoring them as she dusted the contents of the cabinet. "There's a young lady standing near that cabinet and another one at the door who greets your customers. Both entities are calm, and if I had to guess, I would say they are tied to the store in some way."

Darius strained to see what he could not. "Tied

how?"

Jerry wanted to tell him it might be their job to watch over the store but figured it would lead to other questions. "I just meant they seem to be attached to the building rather than an object. I wouldn't know for sure without speaking to them."

"And that could explain the shadows and cooler temps?"

"Most definitely." Jerry looked to see April checking out the window displays. "My family is getting ready to come in. My fiancée doesn't have the gift, so she will key on me when she enters. Her daughter, Max, will key on both the woman at the door and the one at the cabinet."

Darius looked intrigued. "What about the dog? I've heard dogs can see spirits. What will he key on?"

"It's hard to say, but my guess is he'll sniff out the stairs," Jerry said, leaving out the fact the pup would most likely know Gunter had used them.

Darius looked up as April, Max, and Houdini entered.

April keyed on them the moment she entered, smiling at Jerry. Max stopped upon entering, then skirted around the woman standing by the door. Once clear of the spirit, she looked to the right, focusing on the woman standing near the cabinet. The wild card, Houdini, did just as Jerry had predicted. Lowering his nose to the ground, he growled and pawed precisely at the spot where the steps lay hidden beneath the white-speckled linoleum floor.

Darius turned to Jerry. "Okay, I'm convinced. Now what?"

"It would help if I could go down in the basement," Jerry said as April approached.

Darius stepped out from behind the counter and focused on April. "You mind watching the shop?"

April blinked her surprise as Darius started toward the back without waiting for an answer.

"Can we go?" Max asked.

"Sure," Darius called over his shoulder.

Jerry smiled and gave April a peck on the lips. "Have fun minding the store."

"What do I do if someone comes in?" April asked.

"Relax, Ladybug, you've got this. Just smile and welcome them to the store."

"And if they want to buy anything?"

"I'm sure Darius will give you a commission on the sale," Jerry said. "Listen, Darius told me he can hear when someone comes in. If you need anything, stomp your foot three times, and one of us will come up."

Darius was waiting for him at the back of the store with Max and Houdini. He held open a metal grated door, which, if locked, offered no hint of escape. He waved Jerry down a narrow set of stairs that had seen better days and offered no handrails for support. Realizing this had the making of a horror movie, Jerry slid his hand to the back of his pants and felt his pistol before stepping through the gate.

"Max, have Houdini wait at the top until you're down. I don't want you both on these steps at the same time," Jerry said over his shoulder.

"Okay, Jerry."

The floor at the bottom of the steps was no better as the pink and blue tiles crumbled under his feet for the first several steps before firming once more. Unlike the main floor, the basement was obviously used for storage, as it was filled with antique furniture, suitcases, boxes, and plastic storage bins. What he didn't see was any sign of Gunter or the spirit he'd been sent to retrieve. Then again, it may have been because the overhead lights didn't stretch the length of the building. From the stairs back, the basement was eerily devoid of light. Jerry felt the pull and moved forward just as Houdini skirted past. He followed as the K-9 lowered his nose and sniffed his way toward the front of the building and paused when the dog stopped to sniff around the recesses of the staircase.

"Do you see your ghost?" Darius asked as he and Max caught up.

"Not the one I'm looking for," Jerry said. While it felt as if Gunter were near, he couldn't see him.

Darius's eyes grew wide. "Meaning there are

others?"

"Yes, but these seem to be attached to things that are stored here," Max said before Jerry could answer. She pointed at the far wall. "Jerry, he's in the tunnel."

Jerry looked at the wall but didn't see any sign of a tunnel. "Where?"

Max pointed once more. "Over there."

"The tunnels are blocked off," Darius said when Jerry started forward.

"Tunnels? As in more than one?" Jerry asked.

Darius bobbed his head. "Yes, they run under the town. But like I said, they were closed off years ago."

"Why did the town have tunnels?" Max asked.

"A lot of places used tunnels to move coal for heating the buildings," Jerry told her.

"It's true," Darius agreed. "They also used the tunnels to move money between the banks. There was one on each corner, and it was safer that way."

Houdini started toward the wall where Max had pointed. *Max, call Houdini*, Jerry said silently so that only Max could hear. While Darius claimed to believe them, Jerry didn't want to explain how the dog was able to walk through walls.

Houdini stopped his approach and then growled a menacing growl.

"What's happening?" Darius asked as Jerry stepped closer and ran a hand along the dog's back.

"They're coming," Max said softly.

"Who's coming?" Darius's voice held a note of fear mingled with wonder. "Is it the ghost?"

Before they could answer, the man with one shoe appeared through the wall. The spirit took one look at Jerry and turned around. He stopped when Gunter pushed through the wall, blocking his way.

Houdini snarled when the spirit pivoted in Jerry's direction. As if realizing his defeat, the man lifted his hands in resignation.

"He's ready to talk," Max whispered.

Darius sighed. "You mean that's it?"

"No," Jerry said. "We still need to find out what's troubling him."

"I'm going upstairs," Darius said, leaving without further comment.

"Wow, he looks pretty upset," the spirit said. "Was it something I did?"

"No," Jerry said, recognizing the moment for what it was, as he'd witnessed it many times over the years. "It's something you didn't do."

"What didn't I do?"

"You didn't let him see you." Jerry glanced at Max, who nodded her agreement.

Chapter Eleven

Jerry addressed the entity. "What is your name?"

The spirit crossed his arms over his chest. "Puddin n' Tain, ask me again, and I'll tell you the same."

Gunter beat Jerry to the groan.

Max tugged on Jerry's shirt. "That's not really his name. I see a bear—maybe his name's Teddy."

The spirit's eyes grew wide. "How'd you know that?"

Max shrugged. "I told you, I saw a bear. I don't know anyone named Bear, so I figured it must be Teddy."

Teddy eyed Jerry. "I don't like her. She knows too much. Make her go away."

"She's with me," Jerry replied.

"Then I guess we're at an impasse," Teddy said,

crossing his arms.

Jerry looked to Max for direction. “It’s your call, Max. Do you want to stay or go?”

“If you don’t need me, I could go upstairs and see about the other spirits,” Max said. “I know you’re going to want to talk to them anyway, so it might save time if I start now.”

Jerry smiled. “Smart girl.”

“You want me to leave Houdini here?”

“No!” Teddy said, answering for him.

Jerry ignored the spirit. “I’d feel better if you take him with you and not because Puddin ‘n Tain here told you so. If you’re going to speak to spirits, I’d rather you have him near.”

“Okay, Jerry.” Max clapped the side of her leg. “Houdini, heel.”

Houdini moved to Max’s side without hesitation and followed as she made her way through the narrow path. When she reached the stairs, she made the dog wait. Seconds later, the dog raced up the stairs. Jerry looked toward the ceiling as he heard the patter of feet overhead. He lowered his gaze to the spirit. “Satisfied?”

Teddy gave a nod to Gunter. “What about that one?”

“He stays,” Jerry said, leaving no room for argument.

Gunter smiled a K-9 smile.

“Fine, just do what you’re going to do to me and

get it over with," Teddy said.

"What exactly do you think I'm going to do to you?" Jerry asked, leaving out the fact he was incapable of actually doing anything to the spirit.

"I haven't a clue."

"Then why'd you run?"

"Because you were coming for me. I can't run that fast, so I hid in the tunnel. I thought I was safe on account of no one uses those anymore. I didn't know you were going to send in the dog."

"I sent the dog because I wanted to try and help you," Jerry replied.

"Some help you are, sending the dog in after a crippled old man. Even now, you expect me to stand here without so much as a walking stick."

Oh, for Pete's sake, it's like talking to Bunny. Jerry walked to where the antiques were stored and pulled two ladderback chairs free. He placed one facing him and turned the other one around, motioning for Teddy to sit.

Gunter growled when Teddy balked.

"I asked you to sit to make you more comfortable. I'm not going to tie you to the chair," Jerry said. He straddled his chair, using the ladderback as a barrier between him and the spirit. Gunter stood watch until Teddy sat then lowered to a crouch at Jerry's side. Jerry smiled a disarming smile. "Max said your name is Teddy. Was she right?"

"Some call me that. Others call me Theodore. Theodore Johnston."

"Do you know why you're here?"

Teddy peered at Gunter and puckered his face. "Because you sent that foul beast after me."

Gunter growled.

"Okay, let's try this again. Do you know you are dead?"

Teddy's face went slack.

"So, it's safe to say you didn't know," Jerry said sympathetically.

The spirit burst out laughing. "Of course I know, but I had you going there for a moment."

Jerry resisted the impulse to tell Gunter to bite the man. "Listen, I'm more than willing to take time out of my family vacation to try to help you, but these games have to stop."

The spirit wrinkled his brow. "Vacation?"

"Yes, my family and I are here on a trip."

"No, you came here to banish me."

"I'm not following you."

"The heck you aren't. You followed me to this store and had that dog fetch me like I was a varmint."

The man wasn't wrong. "No, I meant I don't understand what you're saying."

Teddy leaned forward and spoke slowly. "Do you not command the English language?"

Jerry reconsidered siccing the dog. He took a deep breath. "Mr. Johnston, why do you think I'm here to banish you?"

"Because you came to Pennsylvania."

"You're going to have to be clearer than that."

Teddy sat back in the chair and crossed his arms. "Word in the Spirit Pipeline was that the great ghosthunter Jerry McNeal was coming to Pennsylvania. Next thing I know, you're knocking on my door. So, of all the towns in Pennsylvania, why do you show up at my door if not to banish me?"

Jerry stared at the entity, mouth agape, trying to process what he'd just heard. He retraced the conversation and realized he'd not told the entity his name. He had so many questions but wasn't sure he was ready for the answers, so he decided to stay the course. "We came to DuBois to return a heirloom to its rightful owner."

"What heirloom?"

"A keepsake that belonged to two ladies who've crossed over to your world."

"That'd be those two lookers that came to the house with you?" Teddy asked.

"Their names are Lina and Elke, and that would be a yes."

"Is it safe to assume they will want to stay with this relic?"

"I hope so. They remained at the house to get a feel for the family before making their decision, but my gut tells me they will stay."

"Hot dang, things are looking up." Teddy's jubilation was short-lived. "Then again, what would fine ladies like that want with an old cripple such as myself?"

Okay, that spirits even worried about hooking up was almost too much to grasp. Then again, being dead hadn't stopped Gunter. Jerry shook off the image and decided to look to the root cause of the man's injury. "How did you lose your leg?"

"I lost it because of the fire."

"Fire?"

"Yep, June 18, 1888. I still remember it like it was yesterday. Nearly lost the town that godawful day. As it was, we lost all but six buildings downtown. It all started because that blasted woman didn't mind her cookstove. The only good thing that came out of the fire was the fire department."

"What fire department?" Jerry asked.

"Exactly."

"You lost me."

"There wasn't one. But that fire woke people up, and the town got its first fire department on June 25 of the same year. I'd have been on it if not for my foot."

"You said you were injured in the fire, but I don't see any burns."

"That's because there weren't none. I didn't get hurt in the fire. I got hurt after—I stepped on a rusty nail while helping clear the rubble. I tried doctoring it on my own until I couldn't bear it anymore. By the time I went to the doctor with it, he said the only thing he could do was take it off, right below the knee. Blasted injury followed me beyond the grave. I used to work in these tunnels, hauling coal to the stores, so I was stuck here hobbling to and fro."

"Then, as luck would have it, I was just on the other side of that wall there the day Ben came to get the shelf. He and that nice man that works upstairs were trying to carry it and I thought to give them a hand. We went up the stairs, through the building, and the next thing I knew, I was outside. I hadn't even thought to try before, and there I was, standing out in the sunshine. I figured since I was out, I'd ride along with that young man and see where he was going. Turns out it wasn't very far, but it was a nice change, so I thought to hang around a bit. Things were going well until I overheard them talking and realized they could hear me hobbling around. Then they were talking about an exorcism. Next thing I knew, I saw where you were coming to town, and I figured you were coming to toss me out."

Jerry sat for a moment, pondering where to start. Finally, he decided to start with the one that would benefit him most. "You said you heard about me through the Spirit Pipeline. What is that?"

"Why, it's where we get our news, of course."

"So exactly what are we talking about? Television? Radio? Newspaper?"

"I guess it's more of a frequency."

"And all the spirits are hooked into it?"

"No, it's more of an opt-in service. If you're tuned in, you get all the gossip."

Gossip was right. Whoever was running the Ghost News Network sure had him pegged wrong. Jerry smiled. "Is there any way of being taken off the mailing list?"

"Now it is I who is not following you," Teddy said.

"Spirits seem to know who I am and where I'm going. Is there any way to take my name off your radar?"

Teddy shook his head. "Not likely. You're a big fish in the pipeline. Spirits want to know where the big fish are. I'm pretty sure that little girl of yours will be added to the list soon. She's got the right stuff."

Jerry didn't like the idea of Max being on any spiritual radar but took comfort in the fact she had both Gunter and Houdini looking over her. "You said your leg affliction followed you to the great beyond. You know that doesn't have to be, right?"

"Sure it does. The leg died before I did and was buried long ago. It's not like it can grow back," Teddy said tersely.

"What happened to you when you were alive happened to your body. You are a spirit now and don't have to remain attached to the body you had here on earth," Jerry said.

Teddy fidgeted in his chair. "You're certain of that?"

The truth was Jerry wasn't certain of anything when it came to spirits, only that wasn't what Teddy needed to hear. "Mostly."

"Prove it."

Great way to put your foot in your mouth, McNeal. Exactly how am I supposed to prove something like that when I don't even know…

Gunter yipped to get his attention.

Jerry nodded. "You know, that just might work."

"What might work?" Teddy asked.

Jerry realized he'd spoken to Gunter out loud and smiled. "You'll see. Go ahead, dog. Give it your best shot."

Gunter groaned.

Jerry realized what he'd said and shrugged his apologies.

Gunter stood, instantly revealing all the wounds he'd received when alive.

Teddy pushed from the chair and stumbled backward. "What happened to that dog?"

Jerry looked Gunter over, his gaze settling on each of the dog's wounds. "Gunshot, knifed, ear bit off by a drug dealer."

"Is he in pain?"

"No more than you are," Jerry replied. "As you can see, the dog had his share of injuries, and yet he chooses not to let them plague him in the afterlife. That's enough, Gunter."

Instantly, all the wounds vanished. The only thing left was the bitemark in his ear.

"Is that proof enough?"

"What's up with the ear?"

Gunter smiled.

"I'm not sure, but I get the feeling he likes showing that one off. From what I hear, the perp got as good as he gave."

"Perp?" Teddy said, returning to his seat.

"Bad guy," Jerry clarified.

"And he can make those wounds come and go on a whim?" Teddy asked, studying Gunter.

"Seems that way." Jerry started to tell him about Gunter's shenanigans at the zombie race but didn't want to have to explain what zombies were if the man didn't already know.

"I don't get it. He's a dog; how'd he know to come back whole, and I didn't?"

And there was the hundred-million-dollar question, and one he had no answer for. "Listen," Jerry said, leaning heavily on the back of the chair. "I don't have all the answers. I just know it is possible, as I've seen it many times."

"So, how does it work?"

Beats me. "Maybe you just have to think about it."

"You think I haven't?" Teddy said tersely.

Gunter growled.

"Easy, fella," Jerry said, hoping the sentiment would settle both man and dog. He pointed at Teddy's stump. "Look at your leg."

Teddy peered at his good leg.

"No, the other one. Visualize it. See yourself as whole."

"It's no use," Teddy said after a moment of silence.

Gunter woofed. Jerry watched as the ghostly K-9's torn ear repaired itself.

"It worked!" Teddy exclaimed.

Jerry thought Teddy was talking about Gunter until he saw the spirit standing before him on two good legs.

Devoid of foot coverings, Teddy wiggled all ten toes against the cool tile floor. "I can't tell you how long I've wanted to do that. I swear, if I weren't a dead man, I'd cry."

Jerry started to tell him being dead didn't prevent him from crying, but decided against it, figuring some things were best left alone.

Teddy took a tentative step, testing his new leg. He then hopped up and down before striking out in a jig. He grinned at Jerry. "Just making sure they're not just for show. Do you think that nice couple will let me stay now that I'm not hobbling all over the place?"

"There's nothing holding you anywhere at this

point," Jerry said. He watched as Teddy walked to the far wall and looked at the slanted shelves that lined the wall. While empty to the naked eye, when the man turned, he was holding a shiny new pair of shoes.

"Ha! First time in ages I get to wear both shoes." Teddy snapped his fingers and then slid a wary glance at Gunter. "I need to grab something. I promise I'll be right back."

Jerry nodded. "Go ahead."

Teddy disappeared into the wall, reappearing a moment later carrying a large box. He opened the flap to show it filled with shoes. "I kept these hidden in the tunnel. It started with one, and then I added to it each year when I bought my shoes. I just didn't have the heart to throw the other one away. I guess it pained me to have to pay for two shoes when I only needed one. I thought maybe one day I'd find a one-legged man that might be able to use them. Silly, I know, but if someone had given me a box such as this, I would have treasured the gift," Teddy said as he offered the box to Jerry.

"You want me to have these?"

Teddy bobbed his head. "You said it's what you do."

Jerry stared at the spirit without blinking. "What I do?"

"You said it's why you came to Pennsylvania, to help spirits. It really would help me if you could find someone to take these shoes."

Don't do it, McNeal. Not listening to his own advice, Jerry took the box.

Gunter groaned and shot him a look that said, "When will you ever learn?"

Chapter Twelve

Max started across the room, half expecting Jerry to call her back to tell her he was just kidding. While she knew he believed in her, when she'd asked if she could try talking to the spirits alone, she'd expected him to tell her to wait for him. Not only had he agreed to let her talk to them, he had seemed happy she'd asked. This was her chance to show him she was ready to do the job, and it was all she could do to walk across the floor without running. He was watching. She knew it but wasn't about to let him know she knew, as any sign of hesitation could give him the wrong impression. She stopped at the stairs and motioned for Houdini to wait. She hurried up the stairs, stopped at the top and smacked her palm on her outer thigh. "Houdini, come."

The shepherd bounded up the stairs, greeting her as if they'd been separated for hours.

Max knelt. "You're just as excited as I am, aren't you, boy?" she said, roughing his fur. "This is our big chance to let Jerry know we can do things on our own. I need you to be on your best behavior and stay quiet unless there's a problem."

Houdini answered with a canine kiss.

Max stood, silencing her phone as Houdini moved to her left side. *Time to go to work*, she said, communicating with the dog via the power of her mind.

April looked up from her conversation with Darius. "How's it going?"

"Good. Jerry sent me to talk to the other spirits." Okay, it was a slight stretch, but it felt good to say it. As she walked toward the front entrance, she heard Darius ask her mother how she could believe in things she could not see. Knowing her mom had her back, Max continued.

Ever vigilant, the woman's spirit stood by the entrance, waiting to greet anyone who entered. She turned to face Max when she neared. "Are you here to tell me to leave?"

Max shook her head. "No, ma'am. Not if you don't want to."

The spirit frowned. "I thought he sent you to do his bidding."

"He? You mean Jerry?"

The spirit nodded. "Yes, Mr. McNeal. We heard he was coming and know what it is he does."

Max sighed. Talking to spirits was harder than she thought. "You've got it wrong. You don't need to be afraid of Jerry. He's only here to help Teddy."

The spirit looked toward the back of the store. "Mr. McNeal is talking to Theodore?"

Max smiled. "Yes."

"We heard he was coming to town and knew he was after one of us."

"That's not true," Max said firmly. "We didn't even know you were here. We came to talk to Mr. and Mrs. Krafft. We wouldn't have known about Teddy if he hadn't made so much noise."

"But now you do, and he's here to collect him."

"No, I told you…"

"He's a ghostbuster, isn't he?" the spirit said firmly. "Do they not collect spirits?"

"Collect spirits? You mean like in the movie? How do you even know about that?" Max asked.

"Ah ha, then it's true!" the spirit spat.

Max stepped back.

Houdini growled and moved in between her and the spirit.

"Max, are you okay?" April called from the other side of the room. "Do you need me to get Jerry?"

"It's okay, Mom. It's just a small misunderstanding." Max took a breath to calm herself. "I don't know who told you Jerry was here to harm you, but I can tell you he's never hurt anyone, living or dead. He's a good guy and came here to help Teddy."

"Lies. You just said you came to talk to someone else."

A tear trickled down Max's cheek. Angry at herself for letting the spirit get to her, Max removed it with the back of her hand and firmed her chin. "Listen, lady, if you want to stay in the building for all of eternity, then that's fine by me. I told you Jerry and I are here to help and it's the truth. Now, you can either talk to me and let me figure out why you are stuck here or not. It's up to you."

"Shirley."

"What?" Max sniffed.

"My name is Shirley." She nodded to the girl standing by the corner cabinet. "That's my daughter Helen. She's the one who insists on staying here while I spend my days standing at this door, hoping one day she'll change her mind. Perhaps that is why you came, to help her let go of the past."

Max stared at Helen, who seemed overly interested in the items on the white corner cabinet.

"I'll do my best," Max promised.

"That's all any of us can do," Shirley replied.

As Max neared, Helen stopped rooting

through the contents of the cabinet. Her gaze trailed to Houdini, who'd practically glued himself to her side.

"Your dog isn't like other dogs, is he?" the spirit said, admiring Houdini.

"No," Max said without divulging more information about the half-ghostly pup.

"I didn't think so. Most dogs yap at us or simply stare in our direction. But not this one. No, this one seems like he understands everything that is said."

Max beamed under the compliment. "That's because he's extra smart. He's a search dog and very good at finding things."

Helen smiled a sad smile. "I wish he could find what I lost."

"Maybe he can," Max proclaimed boldly. "Tell me what you are looking for, and I'll ask Houdini to help find it."

Sadness touched the woman's eyes. "No, the dog can't find what I'm missing."

"Please," Max urged. "Tell me what it is you're looking for."

"It's not a what. It's a who. I'm looking for Roy. He was my husband. I haven't seen him since I…"

Though the spirit stopped talking, Max was able to see her thoughts. The couple was driving in a white pickup truck with rounded fenders. Though the truck was old, Max knew it was brand new. Helen sat next to Roy, who had one arm draped around her shoulder as he drove along a snow-covered two-lane road. The road was riddled with hills and curves. Roy didn't seem to mind, as he kept glancing over at Helen as he spoke. Roy said something to make Helen laugh, and he turned to her, reveling in the joy of her laughter. The road jinked to the right, but Roy wasn't paying attention and the truck continued straight. Somewhere in the recesses of her mind, Helen screamed, and Max's vision cleared.

"It was the last time I saw him," Helen said softly. "I did not survive the crash. I don't know if he lived or died that day. I've been waiting here for him, but he never came."

Max looked about the room. "Why here?"

"I used to work here. Roy worked in the laboratory on North Brady Street. I got off work thirty minutes before him, and I'd hang out here in the store doing odds and ends while waiting for him."

Max turned to face the door. "Why am I seeing a knight sitting on a white horse?"

Helen sighed. "Roy's last name was Knight. He drove a white truck."

The antique store faded into a shoe store with a set of stairs sitting in the middle of the room just inside the door. Helen came up from below wearing a white formfitting dress with red polka dots, a red belt, and matching heels. She looked out the window, saw the pickup truck pull to the curb, and smiled. She hurried to the counter and handed the shoebox she was carrying to a man with greying hair. The man reached underneath the counter and retrieved a red purse and camel-colored coat.

The man set the purse on the counter, helped her with her coat, and then offered her several coins.

She tried to wave him off. "That isn't necessary. I'm the one who chooses to stay past my shift." It wasn't that she didn't have need of the money, but the man had hired her when no one else in town was keen to hire women.

"Take the coins," he said, pressing them into her hand. "You've earned them."

Helen rewarded him with a quick peck on the cheek, then shoved the coins into her pocket.

The man smiled. "Tell your husband I said to keep his eyes on the road. It's been snowing for the past hour, and I want my best girl to make it home safe."

"Roy always drives safe," Helen said. She pulled a pair of gloves from her pocket and slipped them on before retrieving her purse. Her red heels clicked on the tile floor as she hurried to the door, reaching it just as Roy pulled it open.

"Come to me, lady. Your trusty steed awaits."

Helen giggled as she ducked out the door.

Once again, the vision cleared. Max turned and saw Helen messing with the corner shelf once more. "What are you looking for?"

Helen peered at the cabinet.

As Max followed her gaze, the cabinet—or one that looked just like it—sat in the corner of a small room with hardwood floors. Helen stood in front of the cabinet, staring at a small, hinged box.

"Hello, my love," Roy said, coming into the room.

Helen closed the box and hid it behind the crystal vase. "I was thinking about moving this cabinet into the front room." She hated lying to him, but their anniversary wasn't for a few more days, and she didn't want to spoil the surprise.

"Clear it off, and I'll get it done," Roy said, moving up beside her.

She turned to face him. "Not yet. I haven't decided for sure."

He pulled her in for a kiss. "Let me know when you do. Until then, I'm going to add some coal to the furnace." He released her and left the room.

Helen listened for his footsteps on the basement stairs and reached for the box with trembling hands. Opening it, she peered at the cufflinks she'd bought with the coins she'd earned from spending that extra half hour waiting for him.

The lid to the box snapped closed, clearing Max's vision once more.

"Max? Are you alright over there?" April asked, pulling her attention.

Houdini whined.

Max realized the dog had wandered to the front of the store and was now staring out the door. The dog might be half ghost, but he had the needs of a living dog.

Max sighed. No wonder Jerry preferred to work alone. "I'm good, Mom."

"Houdini needs to go out. Do you want me to take him?"

Another sigh. How was she supposed to take care of Houdini and talk to spirits? "I need to take care of my dog. Will you be here when I get back?" Silly question. Of course Helen would be here; her mother said she never left.

Helen turned and began rifling around the shelf without answering.

Max walked to the front and attached the leash to Houdini's collar. After exiting the store, she stood on the sidewalk, wondering where to take the dog to do his business. Houdini, on the other hand, was ready to go.

"Houdini, heel," Max said firmly.

Instead of complying, the dog pulled Max to the corner.

"Houdini? What's gotten into you? If the agency saw this, they'd take away your certification," Max scolded.

Houdini barked and stared at the other side of the road.

"I don't see any grass that way," Max said, tugging the dog in the opposite direction.

Houdini stood his ground.

"What's gotten into you? Why do you want…" Max gulped as she stared at the street sign. "North Brady Street! That's where Helen said Roy worked. Is that what you're trying to tell me?"

Houdini yipped and spun in a circle.

"You know where Roy is, don't you, boy?"

Houdini woofed and wagged his tail.

The light changed. Houdini led the way across the street. They had nearly reached the end of the block when the dog stopped in front of a building on the left side of the street. A sign on the door read "Til Vintage."

Max frowned. "You're saying he's in there?"

Houdini gave a growly yip.

Max looked back the way they'd just come. "But it's so close…"

Houdini barked, drawing her attention.

Max opened the door, and Houdini followed her inside. Several shoppers glanced at Houdini's service dog harness and then went back to what they were doing. Max scanned what she could see of the store, which was cordoned off into sections with posters, clothing, toys, trinkets, and more, as Houdini sniffed at the mannequin that stood guard in the center of the room. While she would love to explore the shop, she was here on business and knew they were on the verge of finding who they were looking for.

A shadow pulled her attention. She sucked in her breath as she watched a small dog fall through the ceiling. She blinked, looked at the ceiling once more, and saw it undamaged. *Okay, that's weird.* Max shook off the vision.

"Are you okay?"

Max looked to see a woman with dark hair watching her. She glanced at the ceiling. "This is going to sound crazy, but has a dog ever fallen through that ceiling before?"

"Who told you?!" the woman asked.

"No one," Max admitted. "I saw it."

The woman furrowed her brow. "I don't recall you being there when it happened."

"No, I mean, I just saw it." She shrugged. "I have the gift."

"You're psychic?"

"Yeah, but Jerry just calls it 'the gift.'"

The woman rounded the counter and pointed to the ceiling. "It actually fell through twice."

Max took in the distance to the floor. "You mean it didn't die?"

The woman laughed. "No, a customer caught it the first time, and the second time, it fell into the chair."

"Why do I get the impression the dog was walking the plank?"

The woman smiled. "It was. The apartment upstairs has a catwalk. No one is supposed to be in the area, but somehow, the dog got in there and fell through. They fixed it after the second time."

Houdini pressed into the side of her leg, reminding her of her mission. "Did this building used to be a lab?"

The woman's eyes widened. "You picked up on that?"

"Yes," Max fibbed. While the woman appeared to believe her, she felt the woman would be less receptive upon hearing she'd been given the information by a spirit.

"I'm pretty sure there was a laboratory."

"I'd love to see it," Max blurted.

The woman laughed. "Honey, I'd like to show it to you, but that lab is long gone."

While Max knew the woman was telling the truth, she also got the impression the lady was holding something back. Suddenly, she wished Jerry was with her. Not that she needed him to do what she came to do, but he could lend credibility to the request. *If only I had a badge*.

Houdini pulled on the leash, tugging his way to the counter.

"My dog thinks there's something left," Max said, hoping it to be true.

The woman eyed Houdini. "Are you trying to say your dog is psychic too?"

Knowing the woman had said it in jest, Max shook off the comment. "Of course not. Houdini is just good at finding things."

The woman stood there for a full moment as if debating. Finally, she walked to the edge of a small room and spoke to a guy sitting on the couch. "Watch the store for a moment." She motioned for Max to follow without waiting for an answer and led the way through a small hallway that looked as if it was used as a sorting room, and into an expansive open space. While the building had probably been something in its heyday, the back part of the building touted exposed ceilings and unfinished walls.

Max sighed her frustration. The woman hadn't been holding back. She wasn't showing Max the second floor because there wasn't one, at least not in this part of the building.

"Check it out. You can still see some of the burn marks from the big fire," the woman said, pointing.

"Cool," Max said, trying to hide her disappointment. *How am I supposed to help Helen if I can't find Roy?*

Houdini pulled free. Nose to the ground, he was off before she could stop him.

"Houdini!" Max called, following.

Houdini stopped in a darkened corner of the

building and barked an eager bark.

Max looked up the small set of stairs that led to a weathered door. Looking to be original to the building, the door was missing a wide sliver section, which allowed a small beam of light to shine in from the other side.

"You're right. Your dog is good at finding things." The woman moved past her and opened the door. While the building they were in was in much need of repair, the hallway at the top of the stairs was updated. The lower half of the walls stood out with deep purple wainscotting as sunlight poured in through windows in and above an oversized teal door. Max's gaze trailed to the door that separated the two spaces, and she sucked in a breath. On the inside middle of the age-worn door was an unpainted wooden inlay with the word LABORATORY spelled out in partially faded letters.

She gasped and covered her mouth.

Houdini smiled a K-9 smile, looking at her as if to say, *Who needs Jerry when you have me?*

Max spun on her heels. When she did, she saw the room as it once was, with sterile white walls and counters. A feeble-looking man wearing a long white lab coat over black trousers stood bent over at the counter, his hand tracing the pages as he read from a thick book. Though he looked much different than in the visions Helen shared, Max knew him to be the man she was searching for.

Roy, she called, using the strength of her mind. *I need to speak to you. It's about Helen. She's waiting for you.*

Roy turned.

Max was surprised to see a man of considerable age with a deep, jagged scar that ran the length of his face.

"We left the door in place because we thought it was a cool piece of history," the woman said, pulling Max from the moment.

Max worked to hide her disappointment. "Can I look around the room to see if I can pick up anything?"

"Another time, perhaps. I have to get back out front."

Max started to object, when Houdini whined a low whine. Roy appeared near the hallway leading back into the vintage store. Still wearing the white lab coat, he motioned for her to follow.

The spirit was waiting for them near the entrance to the upstairs apartments when they stepped outside. Not seeing any other doors, Max wondered if that was the entrance to the purple hallway she'd seen.

"Not here," she said, moving away from the door and into the parking lot that sat adjacent to the building. Once out of earshot of anyone strolling by, she stopped.

Houdini positioned himself between her and the spirit.

"You can see me?" he said without introduction.

"Yes. I've seen Helen too."

"Helen is here? Where?"

"Her spirit is," Max corrected. "She's at the antique store."

"Where?"

Max realized the spirit might not have known about the changes since he'd crossed. "She is at the shoe store waiting for you to come get her."

"Helen's here?" Roy repeated.

"Yes, waiting for you."

His face brightened, then soured once more. "No, she won't be waiting for me."

"But she is," Max insisted. "She doesn't blame you."

"She told you about the wreck?"

Max nodded. "Yes, she said it was an accident."

"No, if she's there, she'll be waiting for the man I once was, not the decrepit old soul I've become," he said sadly.

Come on, Max, think.

Houdini faded in and out.

Brilliant! Thanks, boy! Max said silently. "No, it's not the body she's waiting on. It's the spirit that was attached to it."

"Even the spirit is old," he insisted.

She thought of Gunter and how he was able to morph himself. "You don't have to be, I promise. I've seen it myself. All you have to do is believe."

Houdini woofed.

Roy disappeared as Jerry and Gunter rounded the corner.

Chapter Thirteen

Jerry headed up the stairs, feeling pretty good about helping Teddy. He felt less thrilled that he'd agreed to help find homes for over a dozen outdated shoes. It was doubtful they could pass them off as vintage finds, as none of the shoes had a match. Still, he'd agreed and now carried the box up the stairs. As he pushed through the grate, he saw April pacing the floor and felt her anxiety. He scanned the open room, looking for Max. While he saw both spirits, the girl was nowhere in sight.

"What's wrong?" he asked. "Where's Max?"

"She took Houdini outside. Is Gunter with you?"

Jerry glanced at Gunter. "He's right here."

April's face visibly relaxed. "Okay, then it's probably nothing."

That he hadn't picked up on Max being in

distress kept him calm. “Tell me what it is and let me decide.”

“She went to take Houdini out and hasn’t come back. It’s only been about fifteen minutes, but when I tried to call, she didn’t answer her phone.”

“How many times did you call her?” Jerry asked.

“Seven,” April admitted. “The first time, I called to check on her. But when she didn’t answer, I kept calling.”

While he wanted to tell her she was probably overreacting, she was a mom. Moms were allowed to overreact when it came to worrying about their children. “Hey, listen, I don’t have a bad feeling and she hasn’t called for Gunter. If either she or Houdini were in trouble, we would know. Still, if it will make you feel better, Gunter and I will go look for her,” Jerry said, lowering the box.

“Want me to come too?”

“I think it might be best if you wait here in case she comes back,” Jerry said. It was doubtful that Max would get past them, but not totally impossible. He placed a hand alongside April’s cheek. “Relax. She’s with Houdini. That dog won’t let her get into trouble.”

April held up her phone. “Oh, she’s in trouble, alright. I might even ground her.”

“You can fuss at her for not answering after we know she’s safe.” Jerry lifted the box and took it to the counter.

Darius peered at the box from the other side. "Find something you like?"

"I'm going to check on the kid. Let me know what this stuff will cost me." Jerry placed the box on the counter and hurried to the front of the store before the man had a chance to inspect its contents. Not wanting to waste any time getting a reading, he spoke to Gunter. "Take me to Max."

Gunter raced outside and crossed the street, mindless of the traffic. The dog paused on the opposite sidewalk, looking at him as if to say, *Are you coming or not?*

Jerry sighed, then hurried to the corner and waited to cross at the light. "We need to work on our technique," he said when Gunter met him on the opposite corner. He felt Max's presence the second they started down the street and knew she was near. He'd barely walked half a block when he heard Max yell.

"NO! PLEASE DON'T!"

Gunter started running. Jerry followed, keeping up as the dog ducked into a parking lot.

Max turned to face them when Houdini barked a greeting.

"Are you alright?" Jerry asked, scanning the area for threats.

"I'm fine." Her words held no conviction.

"I heard you yell."

"I was trying to keep Roy's spirit from leaving,"

Max said.

"I thought you were going to help the spirits in the building."

"I'm trying. Roy is Helen's husband. Was," she said, correcting herself. "Shirley is the spirit by the door. She's Helen's mother and won't leave until Helen does. Helen won't leave without Roy. It's a big mess."

"It sounds like it. Hang on. Let me let your mom know you are okay," Jerry said, pulling out his phone. "She's pretty upset."

"She knew I was taking Houdini out," Max replied.

"You've been gone over fifteen minutes. She tried to call, and you didn't answer."

"I put it on vibrate when I was talking to Helen." Max pulled her phone out of her pocket and looked at the screen. "Ten missed calls! I'm not a baby!"

"No, you're not a baby. But we are in a strange town, so your mother has a right to be worried."

"I was working."

"I know."

"And Houdini was with me."

At the sound of his name, Houdini wagged his tail.

"I know, Max. I also know if you had been in trouble, Gunter would have known."

"And Granny too. She always knows," Max told him. "I didn't mean to ignore Mom's calls, but I wouldn't have answered even if I had heard them. You have to tell her how it is. Tell her I can't put a spirit on hold to take a phone call. I have a job, Jerry. The agency is paying me good money, and I haven't even earned it. I know this isn't exactly what they are paying me for, but helping spirits is still my job. No matter what I do, Mom is still going to treat me like a baby."

"It's what moms do."

"It's not fair."

"We'll figure it out," Jerry told her.

"How?"

"I don't know, but we'll find a solution."

"She's going to ground me, isn't she?"

"She said something to that effect." Jerry held up his hand. "Your mom is upset and might say a few things you disagree with. I need you to stay calm until we all have a chance to sit and sort things out. Can you do that for me?"

"I can try."

"No, there's no trying. If you want to be treated like an adult, you need to act like one. I'm not saying you can't be a kid. But if you want to be taken seriously, you'll need to show her you're mature enough to do the job. Understand?"

Max nodded.

"Good. Now tell me what's going on with Roy."

"Houdini, heel." Max waited for the dog to comply, then fell into step beside Jerry. "I thought maybe if I could talk to him, I could convince him to go see Helen."

"How did you know how to find him?" Jerry asked.

"I didn't. Houdini did. He was whining, so I thought he needed to go out. He took me to Roy instead." Max went on to explain about talking her way into the back of the building. She sighed. "It would have been easier with a badge."

"Probably not," Jerry said.

"Why not?"

Tread lightly, McNeal. "Honestly, because she would probably have thought it was fake."

"Because I'm a kid."

"Yes. But mostly because the majority of people don't believe in what we do. That's the reason I don't go around flashing mine. Sometimes it's just easier not to." They reached the corner and waited for the light to change.

"It's not fair."

"You're right, it's not. We won't be able to help them all, but I promise, what we're doing will make a difference to some."

The light changed, and they started across the street.

"I wish I could have helped Helen," Max said glumly.

Just as they reached the sidewalk, Houdini woofed.

Jerry looked to see an early model pickup pull to the curb in front of the antique store.

The ghostly driver tooted the horn, then opened the door and rounded the truck.

Max gasped. "It's Roy! Only his spirit's not old anymore! He looks just like he did in the vision Helen showed me."

Just before reaching the door, Roy stopped and stared in their direction.

Jerry remained quiet as Max and Houdini took the lead.

"You came," Max said softly.

"I cleaned up a little." The scar was gone. Roy lifted his hand, smoothing his slicked-back hair.

"You found the cufflinks Helen's been looking for," Max said.

"They were never lost," Roy replied.

The door to the antique shop opened, and Helen stepped out. "I knew you'd find me," the spirit whispered.

Roy looked at Max. "I had some help."

"Thank you, Max," Helen said, then stepped into her husband's embrace. As he closed his arms around her, both spirits and the truck disappeared.

"I'm proud of you, Max," Jerry said as both Gunter and Houdini moved forward, sniffing the pavement the spirits had just vacated.

Max nodded toward the window where Shirley stood watching them. "Helen's gone. Why is her mother still here?"

"Why don't you ask her?" Jerry replied.

"Are you sure?"

He nodded. "I am. I still have to settle up with Darius. Listen, I hate to rush you, but we should have left town hours ago. I'm afraid we'll have to visit Punxsutawney on the way back. As it is, we're going to miss the wedding, but if we hurry, we can still have lunch and make it to Chambersburg in time for some of the reception."

"Will your friend be mad if you miss his wedding?"

"It's okay, Max; Manning knows what it's like to be on the job." Jerry blocked her from knowing it was a lie. The truth was that not only did Manning not know they were coming, but except for Seltzer, none of his former colleagues knew what he did for a living. While the men knew he had the gift, not all of them would believe him to be the Lead Paranormal Investigator for the Department of Defense. Jerry placed his hand on the doorknob and smiled at Max. "Remember, stay calm."

Max feigned a salute. "Yes, sir."

"Good. You talk to Shirley, and I'll let your mom know you're still working."

Max and Houdini cut to the left to deal with the spirit as Jerry made a beeline to April. "Max is okay. She's on the job and still needs to wrap things up. Can you give her a few moments?"

April looked past him. "Sure."

Sure? That didn't sound like a woman about to tear into someone. He studied April. "You good?"

"Yes, why wouldn't I be?"

Jerry frowned. "I thought you were upset."

"I was scared, Jerry. Moms get that way sometimes. You've been doing this a long time. It's all new to us. I'm sure Max had a good reason not to answer. I understand she's on the job. We just have to set some ground rules. It might take us a little time to adjust, but we'll figure it out. We always do."

Jerry pulled her into his arms. "And that, my lady, is just one of the reasons why I love you. To be honest, I thought I'd have to spend the rest of the day playing referee. Max will explain things when we get on the road. I think you'll be very impressed."

"I'm sure I will." April giggled and nodded toward the counter where Darius sat watching them. "Speaking of explaining things, we can't wait to hear the story about that box. We counted out sixteen shoes—all brand new. I'm not sure why you want them, as they aren't your size, and not one of them has a match."

"Did he say how much he wants for them?"

"To be honest, I didn't ask."

Jerry released her, and they walked to where Darius sat, oblivious to the fact that Gunter had his paws on the counter, sniffing the contents of the box.

"How much?" Jerry said when he neared.

"Nothing."

Jerry eyed the man. "Seems like a strange way to do business."

Darius shrugged. "I price things the way I see fair. Not much need for single shoes, much less a full box of them."

"My granny once bought a single boot thinking to make a planter out of it," Jerry told him.

Darius smiled a knowing smile. "Did she ever make that planter?"

Jerry answered with a grin. "Not that I recall."

"I stand by my price. The truth is, I've never seen that box before, and even if I had, it's unlikely I'd be able to sell them."

"So, no charge?" Jerry said, confirming.

"The only payment I need is hearing the story that surrounds them. I take it there is one."

"There is," Jerry said. "I just didn't think you believed in such things."

Darius leaned back on the stool. "The jury is still out on that, but I do love me a good story, and this has the makings of one."

Jerry was eager to finish up so they could get on the road but knew better than to leave things unsettled, especially since this was Max's first real case. It would be a huge confidence boost if she could help both spirits find peace. He glanced toward the front and saw her speaking with the woman. Leaning against the counter, Jerry crossed his ankles and settled in to tell them about the spirits who inhabited the building.

Chapter Fourteen

Lina and Elke were waiting on the porch when Jerry pulled to the curb. Jerry opened his door and glanced at April, who showed no sign of exiting the SUV. "Aren't you coming?"

"No, I think it best Max and I stay here. We're in a hurry and it will give you an excuse to leave."

"This shouldn't take long," Jerry agreed. Not one to be left behind, Gunter appeared on the sidewalk wagging his tail. The dog led the way up the concrete steps as Houdini barked his displeasure at being left behind. As he neared the house, Jerry saw the sisters.

"We've decided to stay," Elke said as he reached the porch.

Jerry worked to hide his relief. "I'm sure you will be happy here."

"As do we," Lina agreed. "It will be nice to have little ones around."

Jerry rapped on the door. "I'm glad you both have found a home. Just remember, if things don't work out, there is nothing holding either of you here."

"It will be fine," Lina said as the door opened. "That nice man has agreed to allow us to share his home."

Jerry raised an eyebrow. "Ben can see you?"

"Not Ben. Mr. Johnston."

Jerry swallowed. "Teddy's here?"

Lina nodded. "Came home a few moments ago. He looks mighty handsome now that he's cleaned up. Don't worry, there shouldn't be any concerns from Ben and Nicole, as he's quiet as a mouse with that new leg."

The door opened. Ben unlatched the storm door and held it open while Jerry entered. "Your family's not coming in?" he asked, peering out.

"I promised them lunch at Luigi's before we leave town," Jerry said. Looking past Ben, he focused on Teddy, who'd just appeared behind the man. "We are all looking forward to authentic Italian spaghetti and meatballs. I just wanted to stop in to let you know I spoke to the spirit, and things should be quieter from here on out."

"Did you hear that?" Ben said loudly enough to be heard. "Mr. McNeal banished the ghost."

Teddy moved in front of Ben and wiggled his fingers in front of the man's face.

You promised to be nice, Jerry said, using his mind.

"To be fair, Ben started it," Elke said, coming to the man's defense.

Jerry glanced at Lina and Elke, who were now inside listening to the proceedings. "They prefer the term spirit."

"You mean we don't have to move?" Nicole said, coming into the room wiping her hands on a dishtowel.

"Only if you want to," Jerry replied.

Nicole draped the towel over her shoulder and used her hands to cradle her stomach. "Was the spirit angry about leaving?"

"The spirit didn't mean to cause a ruckus. He was missing a leg and walking on a peg. That was the noise you heard."

"Oh, that poor man. I feel so bad now." Nicole frowned. "I didn't know people take their illnesses to the grave. I mean…"

"I know what you mean," Jerry said, cutting her off. "It's normal for a person to take their illnesses to the grave, but they have a choice if they allow that affliction to follow them into the spirit world. Teddy had a choice. He just wasn't aware of that until I told him."

Gunter moved forward, sniffing Nicole's stomach.

As if feeling the dog's presence, Nicole rubbed

her stomach once more. "Mr. McNeal, what a blessing it is that you know so much about the spirit world when the spirits seem to know so little."

Jerry didn't know what to say to that, so he said nothing.

"Mr. McNeal's family is waiting for him. We'd best let him be on his way," Ben said.

Jerry glanced at the three spirits and then directed his comments to Ben and Nicole. "May you all live in peaceful harmony."

Nicole screwed up her face. "All?"

"You, Ben, and the little ones," Jerry said, covering his mistake.

Elke met him on the porch. "Thank you, Mr. McNeal."

"You're welcome, Elke."

"Jerry," she said as he and Gunter headed down the steps. "I know most of the credit goes to you, but I want you to tell April that Sister and I said thank you. The world needs more people like her."

"People like her?" Jerry asked.

"People who are willing to believe in things they cannot see."

"I'll be sure to tell her," Jerry promised.

"Just so you know, we've all pulled together and given her a little gift."

Jerry halted his step. "What kind of gift?"

Elke smiled a sly smile. "A reminder of sorts. It will help us, and besides, she could use a little piece of mind."

Granny appeared at his side as Elke faded from sight. "It's okay, Jerry. It wasn't anything she didn't already have."

"Meaning?"

"You'll see."

Jerry didn't like to be kept in the dark, but since his grandmother didn't seem worried, he decided to let it go. "Where've you been keeping yourself?"

"I've been watching from afar," she told him. "Mostly, I've been keeping Bunny occupied. I thought this job would be easier without her help. I like her, but she's a bit of a handful."

"That she can be," Jerry agreed. "Where is she now?"

"She's at Luigi's saving you a table."

At the mention of food, Jerry's stomach rumbled. "Good, I'm famished."

"Eat quickly," Granny said. "Bunny's been singing your praises."

Jerry turned to ask his grandmother what that meant. The woman was gone. He looked at Gunter. "What was that all about?"

Gunter disappeared and reappeared in the SUV.

Jerry hurried to the driver's seat. The moment he shut the door, he locked it against the unknown.

"You look as if you just saw a ghost," April said. She placed her hand on his and all the anxiety he'd felt only a second earlier melted.

Jerry lifted her hand and kissed the ring he'd placed on her hand when he'd asked her to marry him. It had been his grandmother's ring, one her spirit had insisted he give to April, promising it would help to keep her safe. Now, as he felt the warmth of the ring on April's finger, he knew it was Granny's way of seeing them both safe.

***

Jerry drove the short distance and returned to the metered parking lot that flanked Luigi's Ristorante. A chalkboard sign that read "Chilly with a Chance of Meatballs" sat on the sidewalk in front of the building. Twin red awnings arched over a window to the left and above the single glass door.

Jerry held open the door to the restaurant and waited as April, Max, and the dogs filed inside. The walls and door frames were painted yellow, with hundreds of various-sized framed photos decorating the walls. Not hung in any order, the photos started near the floor and reached to the edge of the cream and green border that outlined a rich blue ceiling. The carpet had a dizzying effect offset by tables covered with diamond-patterned tablecloths. Several groups of people stood waiting to be seated.

"We'll never get a table," April said. "Maybe we should go somewhere else."

"Hello! Jerry! Hello!" a shrill voice sang out.

Jerry looked to see Bunny sitting at an empty table off to the right in the crowded room. She waved her hanky to get their attention.

Max started toward the table.

"Max, honey. We have to wait our turn," April said, stopping her.

A spirit appeared next to the hostess and whispered in the woman's ear. Though the woman didn't seem to notice, she smiled and motioned for them to follow. "Right this way," she said, leading them to the table where Bunny sat.

"I'd ask if you called ahead, but she didn't even ask our name," April said, blinking her surprise. "Seriously, what just happened?"

"Divine intervention," Jerry informed her.

"Bunny's here," Max clarified. She motioned Houdini out of the way, smiling when the dog moved so he was positioned under the table near the front of her chair. "Good boy."

Gunter followed suit, lying on the floor near Jerry as a waitress dressed in black approached the table and placed their drinks in front of them. "Your food will be out shortly," she said and left without another word.

April stared at her glass. "Did one of you order ahead?"

"Not me," Max said, unwrapping her straw.

"Me neither," Jerry replied.

The waitress returned, followed by a man with a tray who stood in place while the waitress went to work placing a white china plate piled high with spaghetti and two fist-sized meatballs in front of each of them.

"I don't know whether to be impressed or terrified," April said, staring at her food.

Though he'd been thinking the same thing, Jerry feigned indifference. "Just one of the perks of the job."

"You mean it's our reward for helping out the spirits," Max clarified, rolling the pasta onto her spoon.

"Are you sure it's okay to eat this?" April asked.

"There's nothing wrong with the food," Jerry said, taking a bite to prove his point. "I'm not quite sure how she pulled it off, but I'm assuming we can thank Bunny for our meal."

"I knew you were hungry, so I took the liberty of ordering for you," Bunny admitted.

Jerry looked up when Max coughed to get his attention.

She's lying, Max said without speaking.

"Max, honey, don't talk with your mouth full," April told her.

Jerry nearly choked on his meatball. His mind whirled as he dabbed at the corners of his mouth with his napkin. *April has the gift.* He glanced at Max, who nodded in agreement. Savannah had once told him she thought it to be the case, but up until now, April hadn't said or done anything to prove her right. *She's one of us!* The thought both excited and mildly terrified him.

April lowered her spoon. "Now what?"

Not wanting to scare her, Jerry worked to hide his excitement. "Max didn't say that out loud. You didn't, right?" he asked, just to make sure he wasn't mistaken.

Max shook her head without speaking. That he couldn't hear her thoughts let him know she'd quickly blocked them both.

April emitted a nervous giggle. "So, you're saying I'm a mind reader now?"

That statement conjured an image of his Uncle Marvin. Though they'd reconciled their differences, he didn't wish to compare April to the man. "No, you're not a mind reader." His words came out harsher than he'd intended.

"Then what?"

Can you hear me? he asked silently.

"Well?" April asked.

Your turn, Max, Jerry said without speaking.

Mom, you know this is a little weird, right? "Did you hear me? Just now, I said this was weird," Max said, speaking out loud.

"No." April sighed and picked up her spoon. "I guess it was a one-time thing."

Jerry wasn't as convinced. "I don't think so."

"Really?" April and Max said at once.

"No."

"But she didn't hear me," Max said.

"Yeah, I didn't hear her," April agreed. "I tried, but got nothing."

"Hello," Bunny said. "You three really should eat your spaghetti before it gets cold."

The color drained from April's face. When she spoke, her voice held a tone of fearful fascination. "Jerry, either one of you is a darn good ventriloquist, or I just heard a ghost."

"Bunny's sitting right next to you. Can you see her?"

April turned to where he'd indicated. "No."

"But you can hear her?"

"Yes, I think it was her."

Jerry looked at Bunny. "Say something."

"What do you want me to say?"

April gasped. "I heard her. She asked what you wanted her to say."

Gunter woofed.

April's eyes filled with tears. "Gunter?!"

Gunter woofed for a second time. "It's nice to meet you too, fella. But you need to keep it down before we get kicked out."

Jerry smiled, and Max giggled with girlish delight.

"What's so funny?" April asked.

"You're forgetting we are the only ones who can hear him," Jerry said.

"Why is this happening?" April asked.

"You're getting ready," Bunny said, then slapped

a hand over her mouth.

A tingle raced up Jerry's spine and settled along his neck. "Ready for what?"

"Oh, my," Bunny said as she disappeared.

April turned to the seat the spirit had just vacated. "Oh my, what? Bunny? Hello?"

"She's gone," Jerry said.

"I don't understand," April whispered.

"Welcome to my world," Jerry said, picking up his spoon.

They ate their meals in silence, each contemplating the ramifications of the new development. Just as they'd finished, both dogs growled.

A heavy energy filled the air. Jerry looked at Max, who ran a hand along Houdini's back to soothe him.

She nodded. "I feel it too."

Jerry raised a hand to get the waitress's attention.

She looked at the table. "Can I get you anything else?"

"We're good," Jerry said, reaching for his wallet. "If you can just bring us the bill."

"It's already paid."

"By who?"

"Mr. Ben. He paid when he placed the order and reserved your table. He added a nice tip as well." She smiled. "He said he owed you for helping save his home."

"I told you Bunny was lying," Max whispered the moment the waitress left.

Bunny could wait. At the moment, all he wanted was to get April and Max into the Durango and head east without letting them know he was worried. "The dogs are unsettled. How about we get on the road?"

Both Max and April stood and headed to the door without arguing.

"You want to tell me what's going on?" April asked when they got outside. "And don't try to sugarcoat it. You've been looking forward to this meal ever since we got into town. I saw you eyeing the desserts when they placed them on the other table. You wouldn't have asked us to leave if there wasn't a reason."

"There is something wrong," Jerry said, ushering them down the sidewalk. "I just don't know what it is."

Both dogs were on alert, but Jerry took comfort in the fact that Gunter was not wearing his vest. As they rounded the building, Jerry sucked in his breath at seeing an array of spirits hovering near his SUV.

Both dogs moved in front of them, hackles raised.

"Jerry!" Max's voice held an edge. "Where'd they all come from?"

"What's going on?" April whispered.

"Spirits," Jerry said.

"As in more than one?" April asked.

"As in over twenty," Jerry replied. "You two wait here. I'll see what they want."

April looped her arm through his. "We're a team, remember?"

"Mom's right," Max said firmly. "There's safety in numbers."

Jerry wasn't sure what the spirits wanted, but it wasn't as if they had any other options. "We head for the Durango. All of us together. If they don't try to stop us, we keep going."

Houdini barked.

"Easy, boy," Max said.

"That's it, nice and easy," Jerry said as they neared the Durango. He'd almost fooled himself into believing they would make it inside without confrontation when one of the spirits moved forward, blocking their way.

Once again, the dogs moved forward, creating a barrier.

"What can I do for you?" Jerry asked.

"Not you. Her!"

For a moment, Jerry thought he was talking about Max, when the spirit pointed to April.

"What do you want with her?" Jerry asked.

"You can't have my daughter," April said boldly.

"Easy, Momma Bear, they're pointing at you," Jerry said, pulling her back.

"Oh?" The word came out in a squeak.

The spirit fully materialized and held out his

hand, showing a gold pocket watch. "I want my grandson to have this."

One by one, the spirits took shape. As they did, Jerry could see each one was holding something. Understanding washed over him. "Did Bunny send you?"

The spirit nodded. "She's been using the Spirit Pipeline to tell everyone about what your lady did to help Elke and Lina. We all have something we'd like returned to our family."

"I'll help if I can," April promised.

"Be careful," Jerry whispered. "It's like strays: You feed one, and they'll tell their friends."

"Good," April replied. "It'll make me feel useful."

It dawned on him that April had given up her job when Max was hired at the agency. He'd never questioned if she missed not working. He smiled. "Okay, Ladybug."

April sighed. "I can hear them. But it would be easier if I could see them."

"I can sketch them," Max said. "I can also make a list of the names and items."

"Perfect," April replied.

Jerry's phone rang. "It's Seltzer. I need to let him know we're not coming."

"We're not going to get to meet him?" April asked.

"Sure, you will. Just not today. It's best to see to

things here before we leave. Don't worry, he'll understand. Gunter will stay here. He's not wearing his vest, so there's nothing to worry about. I'm just going to step aside for a moment to take the call."

"It's okay, Jerry, we've got this," Max said as she and Houdini moved up beside April.

Jerry walked a few steps and clicked to connect the call. "I was just getting ready to call you."

"Take your time coming in. The wedding is off," Seltzer's voice drifted into the phone. "Little Brian swallowed a quarter and they had to rush him to the ER. While they were waiting for it to pass, those two numbskulls convinced the hospital Chaplin to perform the ceremony."

"Yep, that sounds like a stunt Manning would pull. How's June taking it? Something like this can't be good for her wedding book."

"She's fit to be tied. She's so upset that she tossed the whole book in the burn barrel after her third glass of wine."

"Did you bother to remind her that she sent copies of everything in the book to April?"

"I started to, but she was in no mood to be reasoned with. She had two more glasses while watching it burn and is now nursing a pretty good headache. She should be good in a day or two. When she's ready, I'll let her know. Got something to keep you busy for a couple of days?"

Jerry looked to see April and Max confidently

speaking with the spirits that stood before them. Their confidence could be explained by the fact that they each had a ghostly K-9 protector stationed at their side. He chuckled into the phone. "You have enough on your plate without worrying about us. I'm sure we can find something to keep us busy for a day or two."

As Jerry pocketed his phone, he heaved a contented sigh. *Maybe I should just have Fred change my cards to read "Ghostbuster" and just be done with it.*

Coming Fall of 2024

the next book in

the Jerry McNeal series:

Company Business.

Check out
www.sherryaburton.com
for ordering print books, audiobooks, shirts, cups and more.

About the Author

Sherry A. Burton writes in multiple genres and has won numerous awards for her books. Sherry's awards include the coveted Charles Loring Brace Award, for historical accuracy within her historical fiction series, The Orphan Train Saga. Sherry is a member of the National Orphan Train Society, presents lectures on the history of the orphan trains, and is listed on the NOTC Speaker's Bureau as an approved speaker.

Originally from Kentucky, Sherry and her Retired Navy Husband now call Michigan home. Sherry enjoys traveling and spending time with her husband of more than forty years.